ANGEL DUST BLUES

ANGEL DUST BLUES

A Novel by TODD STRASSER

Coward, McCann & Geoghegan, Inc.
New York

Library of Congress Cataloging in Publication Data
Strasser, Todd.   Angel dust blues.

SUMMARY: Feeling increasingly alienated from his
successful and affluent parents, a 17-year-old boy
becomes involved in drug dealing.

[1. Drug abuse—Fiction]   I. Title.
PZ7.S899An   [Fic]   78-31735
ISBN 0-698-20485-9

Second Impression
PRINTED IN THE UNITED STATES OF AMERICA

To M., Dad and Leigh

*And with gratitude
to Ferdinand Monjo*

ANGEL DUST BLUES

ONE

The handcuffs dug into Alex Lazar's wrists. Just seconds before, outside the front door of the Lazar home, the big detective named Dougherty, the one with the red face and blond hair, had clamped the cuffs on him. Now Dougherty and his partner, a small man who reminded Alex of a fox, escorted him down the slate path to the driveway. His hands were locked behind him; the cuffs felt like they were rubbing through the skin and into the bones. But rather than complain and risk being ignored or laughed at, Alex stayed quiet.

Alex looked back at Lucille, the housekeeper, dressed in her bathrobe and standing in the doorway of the big white house watching the detectives take him away. He felt sorry for her, she looked so unhappy. He knew that in a moment she would go back inside and call his parents in Florida and tell them the police had just come to their house and arrested their son for selling drugs. And he knew what his parents would think in a few hours, sitting in the first-class section of a jet flying north, no doubt easing their shock with a few drinks. These detectives

9

were not only taking away their son, but taking away their selfish hopes and dreams as well. Their son would not be the brilliant doctor, the first to discover a cure for, if not cancer, at least tennis elbow. Nor would he achieve any firsts as a brilliant lawyer. Instead he had become the first kid on the block, in the whole community for that matter, to get busted. It wasn't exactly the sort of thing you bragged about down at the yacht club.

In the hedge across the lawn a bird chirped. The sun had not yet risen above the trees, and as the detectives and Alex walked down the path bursts of yellow light flashed between the branches and trunks. Loose gravel grumbled beneath their shoes when they reached the driveway. It was just before 7:30 A.M., and Alex felt groggy from his abrupt awakening by the two cops. It was hard to believe that they were really arresting him. He didn't feel like a criminal. He didn't hate the two men who had rousted him from his bed. It hadn't occurred to him to resist their polite request that he go with them. He had never been in trouble with the police before.

The detectives paused beside their green sedan, covered with a dull film of dew. Dougherty opened the back door. "Okay, Alex," he said, "get in."

The other detective, the fox, got in beside him. With his wrists handcuffed behind him, no matter how Alex twisted in the seat he was uncomfortable. Dougherty got in front and backed the car down the long driveway.

As they moved away from the house, Alex watched Lucille shrink into a tiny dark figure across the wide lawn. With his parents in Florida she was alone in the house. There was no one to stop the police from taking him away. What if he went to jail? he wondered. What if his parents couldn't get him out? Now

Alex felt frightened. That whole year, that whole change in his life had gone out of his control. It was no longer just between him and his absentee parents or between him and his irrelevant teachers or even between him and some of the nerds he went to school with. These men were the police and their idea of punishment was considerably more than losing a week's allowance or being kept after school for detention. In the back seat Alex pushed his knees together so that the detective next to him wouldn't notice that they were shaking.

At the end of the driveway Dougherty stopped the car and looked over the seat at Alex. "According to the law," the detective said, "I have to inform you of your rights. Anything you say may be used as evidence against you. You have the right to remain silent and request an attorney."

Alex nodded. Not that he felt particularly talkative anyway. He sat quietly as Dougherty followed the curving lane past the driveways leading to the various estates in Upper Deepbrook. They passed the rent-a-cop station, drove through the stone gates and on to the road that led to the highway. Alex noticed that the fox was staring at him.

"Where do you think you're going dressed up like that? A goddamn debutante ball?" the fox asked and then laughed.

Alex frowned, not knowing what to say. Earlier, in a daze, he had put on a tie and jacket. Now the fox made him feel silly. It wasn't like they were going to look at his clothes and drop the charges.

"I can't get over this case, Al," the fox said to Dougherty. "Here's a kid who needs to sell dope about as much as the Pope needs birth control. He probably gets more in allowance than I get in salary. Now he gets pinched and dresses up like it's a goddamn party."

11

"Better drop it, Lou," Dougherty mumbled.

But the fox only snickered. "What a house. Front lawn was as big as a football field. What a kitchen. You ever seen a kitchen like that? Two iceboxes, two ovens." The fox turned to Alex. "Who the hell needs two ovens, tell me that?"

They were on the highway now and Alex wished the fox would open the car door and jump out.

"What do you need two ovens for?" the fox repeated.

Alex remained silent.

"Hey, rich kid." The fox reached over and poked him in the ribs. "I'm talkin' to you."

Alex tried to ignore him.

The fox began to look mean. "Hey, Al, looks like rich kid here doesn't think I'm good enough for an answer."

Dougherty looked at Alex in the rearview. "Better give him an answer, Alex."

"But you said anything I say can be used against me."

The fox started laughing. Dougherty looked in the rearview again and grinned. "Don't worry," he said, "we can't use two ovens as evidence against you."

The fox kept laughing. "Jesus Christ, Al," he gasped, "some criminal we got here."

On the highway they approached a school bus, and Alex looked up at the sleepy-faced students inside. In the back of the bus a small group shared a clandestine cigarette, holding it near an open window so that the driver wouldn't smell the smoke. As Dougherty passed the bus a couple of the kids gazed down at Alex without interest. They were just kids. Who ever heard of two full-grown detectives arriving at seven in the morning to arrest a kid? It seemed like a bad joke. He'd only sold some drugs. Who would have thought grown men would get so serious about that? After all, he was only a kid like those on the bus, wasn't he?

Maybe not.

Alex wondered if there was some kind of line you crossed, not in terms of age, but in terms of what you did, that separated you from that great mass of fun-loving young people known as "the kids." If you smoked cigarettes in the bathroom at school, even if you smoked grass in the bathroom, you were still a kid. You didn't see detectives charging into the bathroom stalls to drag out kids with joints in their hands.

But if you sold grass you crossed that line. You were no longer a "kid," you were now a "dealer," as if it took some great sinister effort to sell a drug rather than simply take it. But it didn't. It was deceptively easy to sell a few joints of grass, and from there it wasn't much harder to sell a nickel bag, or an ounce or even a pound.

TWO

Alex could remember a time, back before he'd crossed the line, back when the people he knew—his parents, teachers, friends at school—would have laughed at the suggestion that one day in the spring of his senior year he would be arrested for selling angel dust to an undercover narcotics agent. Not that Alex was such a good kid or great student, but most of those people would have agreed that he wasn't the type to get involved with dealing. Sure, like a lot of the kids around Deepbrook High he now and then smoked a joint, or got a little smashed at a party, but Alex was also the star of the school's tennis team. The year before, as a junior, Alex led the Deepbrook High team to a state championship and he himself was ranked as the second-best high school player in the state. And since the top-ranked player was a year older and would graduate, everyone assumed that Alex would be number one in the state in his senior year.

But early in his senior year Alex dropped off the team and stopped playing tennis completely. Many people had expressed disappointment. Even his dentist had said something, ironically (or was it?) at the very moment he hit a nerve while drilling.

And it wasn't only tennis. Alex had never cared much about grades, but until his senior year he'd always managed a B average. Suddenly he was scraping along with C's or worse. By November of that year people began to say they were concerned about him. On the tests he failed his teachers scribbled notes that they were disturbed by his sudden lack of interest in schoolwork. When his parents flew up from their Palm Beach world of early retirement they said they were worried because he hadn't applied to college. His friends said he looked troubled, and at home Lucille was constantly giving him apprehensive and inquiring glances.

Even Principal Seekamp called him into his office one day in early November just to try and "talk things out." Winter was coming and Deepbrook High was just starting to heat its classrooms. As usual the janitors were having problems with the temperamental heating system and each day the rooms were either much too hot or too cold. That day the school was like a sauna, but as Alex entered the principal's office he knew Seekamp probably still intended to turn the heat on. He slouched down in a chair and watched while the principal dabbed his forehead with a handkerchief.

"Alex," the principal said, "your grades this semester stink."

Alex shrugged.

Seekamp nodded as if he'd expected that response. The principal was a tall, husky ex-marine who still sported a crew cut and whose beard grew so fast and thick that his jaw perpetually looked dark and unshaven. Unlike most of the male teachers, who wore ties, Principal Seekamp always wore

15

turtleneck sweaters under his jacket, something Alex inter-preted as an attempt to make the position of principal appear informal.

At that moment, Seekamp looked about as informal as a boiled chicken

"Christ, it's hot in here," the principal said, pulling off his jacket and putting it on a chair behind the desk. Instead of sitting he leaned against the edge of his desk with his arms crossed as if this too added to the informality he desired.

Alex didn't say anything. He wasn't in the mood to bullshit about the school's heating system. All he wanted to do was get out of that office.

"What are your SAT scores?" Seekamp asked.

"Six forty in math, six hundred in English."

"Where are you applying?"

"I'm not."

The principal wasn't so quick to ask another question. Instead he gazed at the student seated before him. "Alex," he said, the tone of his voice changing to concern, "what do your parents say about this?"

"Not much," Alex said, aware that this was only partially true. His parents had something to say about his not going to college. But they only said it once a month when they flew up to Deepbrook to check on him and the house and run various errands. At that moment, in fact, they were in the house preparing to fly back to Florida that evening.

Principal Seekamp scowled at him. "Alex, do you feel like talking? Can you tell me what's bugging you?"

Alex looked at the man sweating informally in his informal turtleneck while leaning informally against the desk. There was no use in explaining how sick he was of everything, sick of the expectations everyone had for his tennis career, sick of coming to school and studying subjects that had nothing to do with life, sick of his parents' and teachers' naggings about grades and colleges and the future.

What a joke it had been when his mother, after consulting Alex's former psychiatrist, proposed that Alex take the year after high school off and spend a few months visiting "the great museums of Europe," as if a massive infusion of culture was all it took to straighten the wayward kid out. Alex was about as interested in great European museums as he was in learning Swahili. But even if he had been interested in them he would have refused his mother's suggestion. It seemed like he didn't want to do anything his parents wanted him to do. He felt a great need to decide on his own, to be on his own, to think on his own. As soon as his parents said yes to something, he had to say no.

In the principal's office Seekamp was waiting for a reply, but Alex had nothing to say. Not even a good sweaty informal guy like the principal would understand.

THREE

When Alex got home from school that day in November, he was
disappointed to find that his parents had not yet left for Florida.
He went up the stairs quietly, testing his weight on each step,
trying to avoid the squeaky ones. If he was lucky he could
change and get out of the house without parental detection.

He stopped in the bathroom to wash up. A thick, gray edition
of *The American Guide to Colleges* lay on top of the toilet tank.
There was another copy on the Steinway in the living room, a
copy on the glass coffee table near the couches, one on the desk
in his room, another near the pool table in the basement and
still another on top of the television in the den. That was his
mother's new strategy. She'd bought half a dozen of the books
and planted them at well-traveled intersections throughout the
house, hoping that should her son ever feel an inclination to
read up on colleges, the choices would be at his fingertips.

Alex stared at the book. Actually, there was one college that
sounded interesting, Chelonia in New Hampshire. The
brother of a friend of his went there. You had to go for six years,

which seemed like a good idea, especially if you didn't know what you wanted to do afterward. And Chelonia offered all sorts of work programs, foreign travel opportunities, alternative field terms, independent research—everything, it seemed, except schoolwork.

And the school's mascot was a turtle. Alex liked that and he liked the idea of a college where you didn't have to do any schoolwork, but he didn't like either idea enough to actually apply.

After drying his face, Alex picked up the college guide and held it over the open toilet bowl. If his mother found the guide submerged in eight inches of blue-tinted toilet water, would she get a clearer picture of his thoughts concerning college?

From behind him came the sound of someone clearing his throat, and Alex turned to find his father standing in the doorway of the bathroom. He was a stocky man, a few inches shorter than Alex, with shoulders so broad they almost spanned the entire door space. It was his father's habit, when he wanted to talk, to place himself in the doorway so that Alex couldn't get out unless he literally ran him over.

"Looking at colleges?" his father asked, nodding his large, deeply tanned head toward the book in Alex's hand.

"No, I was actually thinking about dropping it in the toilet," Alex answered.

His father smiled feebly as if Alex were making a poor joke. He was wearing his warm-up suit and Adidas sneakers, and Alex assumed he dressed this way so that he could jog straight off the plane and into the Palm Beach playland.

"See any in there you like?" his father asked.

Hoping to gain speedy release from his present confinement, Alex told his father about Chelonia College. But the old man only frowned and didn't move from the doorway. "A turtle for a mascot?" he asked with dismay.

Alex sighed and then flipped the toilet seat cover and sat down. He knew what was coming. On the other side of the bathroom his father had this faraway look in his eyes and Alex did not doubt that he was thinking back to his own college days.

His father, for some absurd reason, was convinced that Alex would go to Columbia, his alma mater. Only the day before he had discoursed through dinner on the advantages of attending an Ivy League school and the advantages of Columbia in particular. Alex had found the discussion amusing. There he was, on the verge of flunking out of school and showing no interest in college at all, and yet his father, almost totally oblivious to his son's situation, talked as if there was no doubt that a second generation of Lazars would enter Columbia that fall and continue from there into a lifetime devoted to laissez-faire capitalism.

"Alex," his father now said, "let me tell you what it was like at Columbia. It was right in the middle of everything." He stared past Alex as if he was reading a script off the shower curtain. "Right there in the center of the action, not hidden out in the mountains of New Hampshire, but right there with the best. Competition—football, basketball, baseball, lacrosse, hockey—boy it was stiff. We played against the best college teams in the world. And the competition didn't end there, son. I had professors who gave two A's a semester, just two, and if you wanted one you fought tooth and nail to get it. The same went for girls, son. When you saw a pretty girl, you knew there were five other guys looking too and you had to outsmart, outdance, outtalk and outkiss every one of them to get her . . ."

As his father continued talking, Alex gradually tuned him out. As a child he had listened attentively, out of politeness if nothing else, to what his parents and other adults said to him. But no more. Now it seemed that about seventy-five percent of what every adult told him was outright bullshit, and his parents were no exception.

Alex was sometimes amazed and even saddened by how strong his dislike toward his parents had grown that year. Especially when for years while he was growing up all he ever wanted was to see them once in a while, to eat dinner with his mother or go to a ball game with his father, or spend a day sailing with him alone. But his parents were always too busy—his father in business and his mother in politics—working too late to eat dinner home, often not coming home until after Alex was asleep. The weekends had been business and politics, too. Alex and his father would take business associates out sailing and Alex would quietly tend the jib while his father talked business. It seemed that his parents liked him best when he required their attention least. Like a car that runs for years without needing servicing, they wanted a low-maintenance offspring.

". . . Now I didn't win every game, son, or get every A or every girl—getting your mother was hard enough—but when I graduated I knew how to fight and how to win when I wanted and how to lose if I had to. Son, the mascot of my school was a lion, and that's just the way I felt that day I walked through those iron gates for the last time. And I'll tell you something, son, there's still lion in me today. Now, all I ask you to do is think about *that* before you go to a college with a turtle for a mascot."

Alex looked up at his father incredulously. Meanwhile his father looked at his watch. There was a plane to catch. His father looked at him again. "Give it some thought," he said. "As a contributing alumnus I've still got some clout over there."

Alex winked at him. "Sure, Dad."

His father smiled, shook an encouraging fist at his son, and turned away.

FOUR

That evening, after his parents left for Florida, Alex drove to the McDonald's in Deepbrook. Michael was outside on the lawn with a couple of younger kids, sophomores, playing Dare—each daring the other to see who could drop a black stiletto closest to his own foot. Alex didn't understand why Michael liked to mess around with the younger kids. He was a tall, gangly guy who stood well above the sophomores, and Alex thought he looked funny playing with them.

But Michael was dead serious. The bet was a dollar and he had just dropped the knife so that the point sank into the grass about an inch from the toe of his sneaker. Michael's young opponent looked a little sick as he reached down, pulled the stiletto from the turf and held it over his own foot, trying to drop it closer than Michael had.

Alex didn't like the game. The year before he'd heard that a kid Michael was playing against had dropped the knife right through the nail of his big toe and had to go to the hospital. Alex thought Michael would have stopped after that, but he didn't.

Now the sophomore was taking a long time aiming the knife.

"Come on, quit stalling," Michael hissed. When he wanted to sound sinister he would talk with his teeth clenched, making a hissing sound as he breathed out the words. "Come on, chickenshit," Michael said, baiting the sophomore who still had not dropped the knife. "If I want to see chickens I can go to the supermarket."

Alex watched as the sophomore moved the stiletto slightly and then let go. It stuck upright in the ground about an inch and a half from his foot.

"Aw, shit," the sophomore cursed as if he'd wanted it to fall closer, but Alex and the others had seen him purposely aim wide.

Michael made the sophomore pay up and then carefully wiped the dirt off the stiletto's blade and put the knife in his pocket. He and Alex got into Alex's BMW and drove around smoking a couple of joints. They had no plans for the evening except to get stoned, and after a while they stopped at Nathan's to play Pong, a video tennis game. As with Dare, Michael played Pong with a concentrated intensity that would have awed world chess masters. Hunched over the controls, his long unkempt hair hiding his face except for a cigarette hanging out of the corner of his lips, he could beat anyone. Alex was one of the few kids who played well enough to make the game interesting for him.

"Listen, you want to split a key with me?" Michael asked. He had just won for the fifth time that night and Alex was reaching into his pocket for another quarter. When you played with Michael, losers always paid.

"A key?" Alex asked.

"A kilo, dummy."

"Of grass?"

"No, of cow manure, what do you think?" Michael said impatiently.

"Wait a minute," Alex said. For about a month he had been selling nickel and dime bags of grass made from ounces he bought from Michael, who used to sell them at school himself until he dropped out. It had never occurred to Alex to buy larger quantities and sell the ounces himself, but he was sure he could. Some of the kids had even asked him for ounces. Alex felt a rush of excitement. A whole kilo of grass. Fat City. "How much?" he asked.

"Seven hundred," Michael said. "You got half?"

Alex nodded. He had a couple of hundred from the deals he'd made that month and he could take the rest from his father's drawer, sell the ounces and replace the money long before his parents came up from Florida again.

FIVE

The next morning Alex drove into town. It had turned colder overnight, but Alex found Michael waiting outside the small wooden house where he lived with his mother. Michael was wearing only his tattered denim jacket over a black T-shirt. He was shivering when he got in the car.

"Fuck, it's cold," he said, rubbing his hands together.

"You should have waited inside, Michael," Alex said. "I would have come in and gotten you."

Michael didn't answer him. Whenever Alex said anything about Michael's house or his mother or where he lived, Michael ignored it. Instead he told Alex to drive to Brooklyn. His connection for the kilo of grass was there.

On the way they smoked a couple of joints and listened to the FM radio. Michael's head bounced up and down to the music and with his hands he played out drum rhythms on his lap.

"Hey, you in the yearbook?" Michael asked between songs.

"Sure," Alex replied.

"Well, what are *you* most likely to do?" Michael asked with a chuckle. That year the yearbook editors had revived the old tradition of "most likelies." It was just another indication of how preoccupied with the future everyone had become. Before senior year nobody ever thought about the future. The most anyone said about it was they wished it was summer so they could go to the beach or they wished it was winter so they could go skiing. But then senior year had reared its tasseled head and suddenly everybody was talking about the future, *the future, THE FUTURE!* Like there was no yesterday or today.

"They say I'm most likely to play tennis in the U.S. Open someday," Alex said. It had started out as an earnest prediction by the yearbook editors, but now it was at best a dubious speculation.

"Yeah, well I was thinkin' about it," Michael said. "You know they never asked me."

"You're not in school anymore," Alex said.

"What do you mean? All they have to do is look behind the utility garage," Michael said. When he wasn't in the city Michael spent most of his time behind the utility garage at school, smoking grass or cigarettes with his old school buddies. "Anyway, you know what I figure I'm most likely to be by twenty-one?" he asked.

"What?"

"Dead."

For a moment Alex was shaken, but then he told himself this was just Michael trying to shock him. He should have been used to it, but Michael had a knack for catching him off guard.

"Like, Michael Martin, most likely not to see his twenty-first birthday," Michael said. "Or, Michael Martin, most likely to become a terminal statistic. Or, how about . . .?"

"Okay, cut it," Alex said, not seeing the humor, if there was any.

27

Michael grinned at Alex in that half insane gleeful way of his. "Listen, man," he said. "The Great Nothing has it all planned."

Now Alex smiled.

Only Michael could have invented the Great Nothing in the sky. He had moved to Deepbrook in the eighth grade and from the first day in school he created a reputation for himself as tough and rebellious and something of a bully. Alex thought it must have been difficult for Michael, being a poor guy in a school filled with well-to-do kids, some of whose fathers were among the second-string famous. There were a couple of famous mothers, too, including Alex's mom, who had been one of the few female county executives in the whole country. And even though she was now temporarily out of politics, she was still a minor celebrity and an occasional talk-show guest.

Michael had no father as far as Alex knew, and he wasn't sure what Michael's mother did. Michael never talked about her, except once when he complained that she'd burned a hole in one of his T-shirts ironing it.

At first Michael was a curiosity to Alex as they got to know each other the summer after their junior year. He was exciting and seemingly dangerous and he stimulated Alex like a fast car or an exotic drug. Alex liked Michael's other-side-of-the-tracks (he actually came from the other side of the expressway) reputation. He liked how Michael had not been afraid to drop out of school and how he openly refused to be herded along from high school to college like the rest of the kids. It was sometimes hard to put into words, this feeling of not wanting to do what everyone else did, of not wanting to be just like all the other kids. But Alex knew Michael felt it, too.

Sometimes he and Michael would stay up all night, smoking

cigarettes and joints, driving all over the place listening to music and looking for new spots to watch the sun rise. Alex did poorly that summer in the few tennis tournaments he entered. After all, it was exhausting to stay up all night and then play two tennis matches the next day. That was when people got concerned, of course. Alex could have joined the Hell's Angels and it would have been all right as long as he won his share of tournaments.

As Alex got to know Michael he began to see where the tough act ended and where the real person began. He soon realized that despite how ornery Michael could sometimes be, the kid really wanted Alex to be his friend. Like on the night he discovered the Great Nothing.

That night they had driven to Montauk, the easternmost tip of Long Island, and built a fire in the dark on the stony beach by the lighthouse. Michael was tripping on acid, but Alex was just stoned on grass because one of them had to stay quasi-rational in case the cops chased them away. Sometime during the night Alex had fallen asleep on the rocks, and when he woke around 5:30, just as the sun was beginning to turn the sky light, he found he was alone.

For a second he feared that Michael had gotten lost or tried to swim to New Zealand, but then he saw his friend standing waist deep in the Atlantic, still wearing his jeans, T-shirt, and the tattered denim jacket. Alex went down to the water and yelled, but Michael pretended not to hear him and Alex finally had to take off his pants and shirt and wade out to his crazy friend.

The Atlantic was cold, and when he got out there he noticed that Michael's lips were sort of blue and the skin on his fingers was shriveled up as if he'd been in a bathtub too long.

"Hey, Michael, I think you're cold," Alex said.

But Michael stood still in the water, facing the wide Atlantic as if he was mesmerized. "There is a Great Nothing in the sky," he said.

"Yeah, what does he look like?"

"He looks like nothing," Michael said.

Alex considered his whacked-out friend for a moment. "Okay," he said, "I get it. Now come on out before the Great Nothing gives you a great cold."

"He is . . ." Michael said, but failed to finish the sentence.

"He is what?"

"He is nothing."

That was fine with Alex, who had been an atheist since he was old enough to know that other people believed in God. He had always assumed Michael was an atheist too. It was hard to think of Michael believing in a god, unless of course, it was this god of nothing.

Later, after Alex had finally convinced him to return to the beach and had rekindled the fire to dry his clothes, Michael grew sad and suddenly turned to Alex and said, "I was waiting out there, man. I wanted to see if you'd come and get me."

Alex waited for him to say more, but Michael just sat there on a rock in his underwear and stared at the fire until he started to cry. Alex knew acid could do that to you. You could be laughing hysterically one minute and bawling the next, but Michael wasn't being hyper or manic like an acid freak. He just cried softly, wiping away the tears as they formed in the corners of his eyes.

Later, after he'd stopped crying, Michael asked Alex if they were friends.

"Sure," Alex said. "What's wrong?"

But Michael shook his head and wouldn't say more. After a while he got into his damp clothes and they drove all the way home in silence. Alex figured Michael would never talk about that morning again. But every once in a while Michael mentioned the Great Nothing, like when he wanted something to happen and only a force like a god could make it happen. It seemed crazy, but Alex also started doing it. His whole life there'd always been someone—Lucille, his tennis teachers, his psychiatrist, even his parents as a last resort—to whom he could turn for help. But when the change started he couldn't go to any of them, and by his senior year, whenever things got really tense, he, too, found himself looking for the Great Nothing in the sky.

SIX

In Brooklyn Alex parked the BMW across the street from a low brick building and turned to Michael.

"A bakery?"

"This is the address he gave me," Michael said, tugging nervously at his hair. Alex looked at the piece of torn loose-leaf paper on Michael's lap and then back at the sign outside the building, G. Schapmann and Sons, Bakers.

"Is that a three or an eight?" Alex asked, pointing at the paper.

"Uh." Michael squinted. It wasn't even 10 A.M. but he was already wrecked from the joints they'd smoked. "It's a three."

"Then it's one of those places," Alex said, indicating a row of decrepit-looking houses across the street from the bakery and wondering if Michael was enough in control to handle this deal.

"Yeah." Michael reached for the door handle.

"Michael?"

"What?"

"Don't you think you ought to take my half?"

"Oh, yeah." Michael reached toward Alex, who laid seven

fifty-dollar bills in his hand. Then he started to get out again.

"Michael?"

"Yeah?"

"Don't give him the money unless you've got the grass in your hands."

Michael smirked. "If I needed advice I would have brought my old lady along." He turned away from the car and headed toward the row of old houses. Alex watched as he knocked on a door and spoke to an old woman who shook her head and pointed to the house next door. Alex imagined Michael saying, *Excuse me, ma'am, is this where the man who sells kilos of marijuana lives?* and the woman saying, *No, sonny, he lives next door.*

Michael went into the second house. Several minutes passed and then he returned, but instead of carrying a package of grass, he was followed by a big, wild-looking black man with very long black hair that fell in curly braids past his shoulders. The man's beard was also braided and he wore chains and necklaces. Michael got into the car while the man stood outside, smiling at Alex through the window.

"He doesn't have it," Michael said. "He says he'll take me into the city to get it."

"Alone?" Alex asked.

Michael nodded. Alex knew they were both thinking the same thing—man takes Michael away and robs him. He looked at skinny Michael and then at the big black man, who must have weighed more than two-hundred pounds.

"What do you think?" Alex asked.

Michael shrugged.

"Let me see." Alex got out of the car and he and the black man shook hands.

33

"Dey call me Chicken," the man said in an accent Alex did not recognize.

"Hi," Alex said.

"You go?" Chicken asked.

"How about if we both go?" Alex asked.

Chicken frowned. "No good," he said.

"How come?"

"Two of you an' one of me," Chicken said, shaking his head. "For de weed all you need is one of you and one of me, see?" He smiled.

Without knowing why he was doing it, Alex looked at Chicken's hands. Each was as big as a baseball mitt. He got back into the car.

"What do you think?" Michael asked anxiously.

"The truth?" Alex asked.

"Yeah."

"Chances are pretty good he's just a big nice guy who'll do us a good deal," Alex said. "But, personally, I wouldn't walk around the block with him."

Michael was quiet for a few moments. Then he pushed the door open and said, "If I'm not back in two hours call the cops."

The kid had guts.

Alex finished a cigarette and turned off the car radio. He glanced at the clock in the dashboard and then down the empty street. Michael had been gone for an hour, he thought, beginning to feel nervous. What if Michael didn't come back? Could Alex call the police and tell them a huge black man named Chicken had stolen the seven hundred dollars they had intended to buy a kilo of grass with?

He lit another cigarette. Not anticipating the delay, he had skipped breakfast that morning. Now he was hungry. To pass the time he got out and walked up and down the block, pausing to look at an old white Porsche parked in front of the bakery. The car was in mint condition, but Alex knew it was older than he. Someone took good care of that car. The black leather seats looked almost new and the wood veneer on the instrument panel was polished. Alex noticed a Village of Southampton beach sticker on the windshield.

His stomach grumbled and he knew it would start to hurt if he didn't put something in it. The bakery was the only place around that looked even remotely promising. He went in.

Inside it didn't look like any bakery he'd ever seen. There were no display cases filled with breads and cakes, no ladies in white uniforms. Instead Alex found himself in a small lobby. There was a reception desk, but no secretary. On the couch to his left a girl sat reading a magazine. Alex walked over.

"Uh, excuse me."

The girl looked up. She must have been around his age. Her hair was black and her eyes dark. Alex blinked. She was pretty.

"Do you know how I can get a Danish or something?"

The girl smiled. "This is a commercial bakery," she said. "They don't sell to individuals."

"Oh."

"But, if you really want one."

"Well, it's not like I need one," Alex said. "It's just that I skipped breakfast and I figured I could stop here."

She stood up and he saw that she was tall and thin. Maybe she was some kind of model, he thought. Maybe they took pictures of her holding rye breads or something.

"Wait here and I'll see what I can get you," she said, walking toward the door at the rear of the lobby.

"I wouldn't want you to go out of your way," he said.

"No problem." She was gone.

He looked at the magazine she'd been reading: an *Atlantic Monthly*.

She returned a few moments later with two pastries wrapped in wax paper.

"Here." She handed them to him.

"Thanks a lot." Alex reached into his pocket. "Can I pay you?"

The girl shook her head.

Alex suddenly wanted to stay and talk. "Uh, do you work here?" he asked.

"No, I'm just waiting for someone."

"Oh." Alex couldn't think of anything else to say. He waited a moment to see if the girl would say more, but she didn't.

"Well, thanks for the pastry," he said, stepping backward toward the door. She watched him with an amused expression on her face. "Well, uh, thanks again," he said just as he bumped into the door.

"You're welcome again," she said.

Alex turned and went outside in time to see Michael and Chicken return in Chicken's beat-up old Chevy. Michael got out and hurried to Alex's car carrying a brown paper bag.

"You got it?" Alex asked when Michael got in. He suddenly felt the nervous thrill of doing something exciting and illegal.

"Yeah."

"Let's see."

Michael put the bag on the floor and opened it. Inside was a flat white sack about the size of two volumes of the

36

Encyclopaedia Britannica. Alex reached in and touched it. The sack felt hard.

"It's really packed in there," Alex said.

"Yeah, it hasn't been opened since it was packed and sewn up," Michael said.

"You try some?" Alex asked.

"Yeah, it's dynamite, look." Michael reached in and turned the kilo on its side and showed Alex where it had been slit open. He pulled out a little grass and handed it to Alex. It was greener and stickier than any grass Alex had ever seen.

"Why's it so sticky?" Alex asked.

"That's the resin, dummy," Michael said. "This is super fresh, super pure grass."

Something moved across the street and Alex looked up. The girl from the bakery and a younger girl who had the same black hair and eyes were climbing into the Porsche. An older man was already inside the car. When the girls were both inside, the Porsche drove away and Alex read the license plate: GSS-22. Did the GSS stand for G. Schapmann and Sons? he wondered.

"Come on, man," Michael said impatiently, "let's go."

Later, heading east on the Long Island Expressway, Alex spotted the Porsche several cars ahead of him in the left lane. He had to exit for Deepbrook before he could catch up.

SEVEN

Alex was a sort of semi-jock who liked sports but who wasn't into the total I-Am-A-Body-And-I-Play-Games jock mentality. He was tall, built leanly and fair (almost the exact opposite of his father), and did not suffer the normal adolescent male insecurities about the opposite sex. In the girls' room at Deepbrook High he was sometimes referred to as a "hunk" and occasionally as a "lust object." In general he didn't have much trouble getting a date.

For two years he had gone with Fran Jamison, the most perfect, most-all-around-goody-two-shoes-brown-nosed-president-of-everything and volunteer-for-everything-else in the class. Together the tennis star and the girl with "the most" had been a popular couple and they rarely missed a party or dance. But as Alex got older he had to add two other "mosts" to those that described Fran. First, she was the most prudish girl he knew and wouldn't even let him touch her breasts. Second, by the end of junior year she had become the most overbearing girl he knew.

They finally broke up. The ciaos got to him.

Ciao means good-bye in Italian, and one night at the end of a routine boyfriend-to-girlfriend telephone call, Fran said "Ciao" instead of "Good-bye."

"What?" Alex said.

With a tone of slight exasperation, Fran explained what ciao meant. Alex thought it was pretty dumb. After all, it wasn't like Fran was fluent in Italian or anything, and even though she was nearly fluent in French, she had never ended a phone call with "Au revoir."

But the ciaos didn't disappear. Instead they multiplied. Soon each time Alex and Fran separated—in the hall at school, after a date, or at the end of a phone conversation—Fran said ciao as if this were the password to sophistication. Maybe it was, but all it did to Alex was get on his nerves. Finally, when Alex felt so ciaoed out he couldn't take it anymore, he started saying sayonara each time Fran said ciao. Sayonara is Japanese for good-bye. He only had to say it a couple of times before Fran got the message. Not only did she stop saying ciao, she stopped speaking to him altogether.

Despite the excitement of buying his first kilo, and all the chores he and Michael had to perform on it, like dividing it up and weighing out ounces, wrapping each ounce in a plastic bag, and hiding all of them, Alex spent most of the day thinking about the girl from the bakery. Almost instinctively he knew that she would never end a conversation by saying ciao. He also knew he wanted to see her again.

Logically, there should have been no way for him to find out who she was, but Alex had a hunch—the GSS in the Porsche's license plate, the name of the bakery being G. Schapmann and Sons, the Village of Southampton sticker. That night after dinner he called Southampton information and asked for the number for G. Schapmann. As the operator read him the number, Alex smiled. Sherlock Holmes would have been proud.

He dialed. "Hello?" A girl answered. Alex felt his heart rev up as if someone had stepped on his accelerator.

"Hi, my name is Alex Lazar and I think we met at your dad's bakery today. Do you remember?"

"Oh, I'm not sure. What do you look like?"

"I'm tall," Alex said. "I was wearing blue jeans and a green down jacket."

"Are you a driver?"

"Uh, well, I have a license, if that's what you mean."

"No, I meant, do you drive a truck for my father?" the girl said.

"No, I don't have anything to do with the bakery. I just stopped in looking for something to eat. You got me two pastries, remember?"

"No, but maybe Ellen did. She's my sister."

"Oh, could I speak to her?" Alex asked.

"Umm. She's reading."

"And you think she doesn't want to be disturbed? I could call back later."

"No, don't do that. We're not allowed to talk on the phone after eight o'clock."

"Oh, well, could I leave a message or something?"

"I don't have a pen," the girl said.

"You know," Alex said, "I get the feeling you don't want me to talk to your sister."

"She doesn't really know you, does she?" the girl said.

"That raises two important points," Alex quickly replied. "One, how do you know she doesn't want to get to know me?

And two, if she doesn't, she can hang up on me just as easily as you."

"I guess."

"Now how would you like it if you met Prince Charming and he called up and Ellen wouldn't let him speak to you?"

"You think highly of yourself, don't you?" the girl said.

Alex sighed. "Please let me talk to your sister. I promise my intentions are honorable."

"Wait." She must have put her hand over the receiver, but Alex could hear clearly as she yelled: "Ellen, there's a stranger on the phone who insists on talking to you. Can I tell him you're not home?"

"Hello?"

"Hi, Ellen?"

"Yes, who is this?"

Alex introduced himself and explained how he found her telephone number.

"Oh." She sounded surprised. "I've never been traced before."

"It was a lot easier than getting your sister to let me talk to you," Alex said.

"Did she give you a hard time?"

"You could say that."

"Well, I hope you'll forgive her," Ellen said. "She's very protective for a thirteen-year-old."

"Does she chaperon your dates?" Alex asked, hoping Ellen would say something to indicate that she wasn't dating anyone at the moment.

The pause on the other end of the line indicated that Ellen was probably considering the implications of the question. "I suppose she'd find them boring," she said finally.

Alex interpreted her answer as meaning she was going out,

41

but not with someone she really liked. In the ensuing conversation each learned that the other was a high school senior and that their mutual interests included movies, theater, sailing, tennis, and skiing. Their views diverged on music (she liked classical, he preferred rock) and politics (she was involved while he couldn't have cared less). The conversation lasted the better part of an hour.

"Alex," she said suddenly. "It's eight o'clock. I have to get off."

"That's the same line your sister gave me."

"It's true. Poppa makes us get off at eight."

"Well, uh, I was wondering if I could see you sometime."

"I don't know, Alex. We hardly know each other."

"We could meet on neutral territory," Alex said. "I promise to come unarmed."

She giggled.

"What do you say?" Alex asked, trying not to sound too eager and failing.

"I don't know," she said. "I've never done anything like this before. I hardly remember what you look like."

"I look like Robert Redford," Alex said.

"No, you don't."

"I know," Alex admitted. "But I was hoping that if you really didn't remember you'd believe me."

She laughed. "I really have to get off, Alex. Why don't you call me again?"

"Sure, what time are you getting up tomorrow morning?"

Ellen only laughed again and said good-bye. Alex knew he would not call in the morning. Rather than chase too hard, he would wait a few days.

EIGHT

During lunchtime on Monday Alex arranged to sell three of the ounces he and Michael had broken out of the kilo. At forty dollars an ounce, or about twice what Alex had paid, the kids thought they were getting a good deal. Alex had given away several joints and the response was unanimous: the grass was potent. Two people could easily get blown away on a single joint.

Thinking his friend James might like to try some of the grass, Alex visited the library. For reasons Alex did not fully comprehend, James, who'd always been an A student anyway, was spending an inordinate amount of time in the library lately. Alex spotted his friend's head of curly black hair behind a small mountain of books at a table near the rear of the book stacks and went over. James was so immersed in his studies that he didn't even look up from behind the pile of books to see who had joined him at the table. Alex waited a few moments for James to finish reading, but his friend still gave no sign of acknowledgment.

"James," Alex whispered.

No answer.

"Hey, James," Alex hissed more loudly.

"Hmmm."

Alex stretched up and looked over the pile of books. On the other side James's head was propped up on several volumes. He'd been sleeping. "Gee, James, what are you reading about?" Alex asked sarcastically.

"Conservation of energy," James mumbled, rubbing his eyes.

"I thought you've been in here studying all these weeks."

James scratched his head, buried somewhere beneath a thick tangle of black curls. "I have," he said and yawned.

"What subject?" Alex asked.

"Her." James nodded toward a girl seated at a table nearby. She had long blond hair and a pretty face. Her skin was tan—an oddity around Long Island in November, being too late for sunbathing and too early for the Thanksgiving rush to the Caribbean.

Alex had never seen her before. "Where'd she come from?" he asked.

"Transferred from Florida last month," James whispered.

Alex rose halfway out of his chair, suggesting they introduce themselves.

James cowered. "No, Alex, please."

"Don't you want to meet her?" Alex asked. "She probably doesn't know anyone here."

"Yes, no, I can't," James mumbled and reached over and pulled Alex back into his chair.

"Why?"

"Basic genetics," James said wistfully.

44

"Genetics?"

"Precisely," James said. "Look at you, tall, good-looking, coordinated, athletic. Look at her, the same adjectives apply. So of course you want to meet her, it's merely the attraction of one gene pool to another, the promise of creating more of the same. Biologically you make sense. In physics opposites may attract, but in biology like likes like. Now look at me." James pointed to himself lest there be any doubt. "Short, funny-looking, uncoordinated. I look at a girl like that and my brain says 'Go, go, go' but my genes say 'Stop, stop, stop.' She and I are a biological mismatch, Alex, so forget the introductions."

Alex looked at the girl and then back at James. "That is the most imaginative excuse for shyness since you said you couldn't ask Terry Clarke for a date because you were having a biorhythm crisis."

"All my waves were below the critical point," James insisted. "By the time they were back to normal she was going with Gilbert."

Alex let the discussion end, knowing there was no way he could get James to meet the girl. For every girl there were fifty reasons why James could not ask her out. Besides genes and biorhythms there were Rh factors, blood types, height problems (at least half the girls in the class were taller than James), and a dozen other purely scientific as well as ridiculous excuses. It was unfortunate that James was short and had a large hooked nose and many splotches of acne present and past, but he also had the deepest blue eyes Alex had ever seen on a guy and if he ever cut his hair, or at least trimmed it, he would have been halfway attractive. Besides, he had to be the most intelligent and entertaining person Alex knew. That had to count, too.

45

James was one of the few friends Alex had made since the change had begun. Even though they were both on the tennis team and had known each other for years, they had never been friendly before. James wasn't a good tennis player. He wasn't even average. On the team he was perhaps best known for the maniac soliloquies he delivered on the bus returning from tennis matches he rarely played in. Covering a range of topics from the possibility of world takeover by walking catfish to detailed accounts of the nighttime activities in his neighbor's bedroom, which he regularly followed through his telescope, James was regarded by most of the team as amusement for the long bus rides home. But as Alex had changed he found he understood the noble gnome's nuttiness. More and more often, lately, when he wanted someone to talk to, he sought out James.

Alex slipped a couple of joints into the pocket of James's perpetually wrinkled blue shirt.

"A present?" James inquired.

"A gift of fresh grass just broken out of the kilo yesterday," Alex said.

James regarded Alex with eyes full of awe. "A kilo as in kilogram? One thousand grams? Or, in deference to metric conversion, two point two pounds of pot?"

Alex nodded.

"How does one go about obtaining marijuana in said quantities?" James asked.

Alex told him about the trip to Brooklyn.

"Imagine," said James, somewhat enviously, "danger, excitement, and forbidden treasure all in one morning. It certainly beats the Sunday *Times* crossword puzzle."

"Oh, and I forgot to mention the mysterious and beautiful woman I met while waiting for Michael," Alex added.

"Really?" James asked.

"Really," Alex said. "I hate to tell you, James, but this girl is incredible. I just hope I'll get to see her again."

James seemed to grow melancholy. "Why do you have all the luck?" he sighed. "I'd give up the danger, the excitement, the forbidden treasure all for one, just one, incredible girl. In fact, I would compromise for a credible girl. I would even settle for a slightly-less-than-credible girl. Actually, given the opportunity I would avail myself upon a completely *un*credible girl."

Alex looked at the girl from Florida again. "She looks pretty credible to me," he said to James.

His friend nodded. "To you perhaps, but to me she goes beyond credibility."

"To what?" Alex asked.

"Total intimidation," James said glumly.

NINE

Getting into the White House to see the President of the United States probably wasn't as hard as getting a date with Ellen Schapmann. Alex called her back, in fact he called her several times and they had long enjoyable conversations. But each time Alex asked to see her she demurred, saying only that she hoped he'd call again.

The entire month of November passed on the phone. Alex waited for Ellen to tell him she had a boyfriend, but she didn't. In subtle ways she encouraged him to keep calling. Then one day in early December, out of the pure blue—or pure gray, considering the miserable weather—she called and said she had two tickets to a Saturday matinee on Broadway. Would he like to meet her there?

Why not? Alex said, as if it was every other week that the girl of his dreams called and asked him out.

They had agreed to meet outside the theater at 1:30. Dressed in a tie and jacket, Alex arrived a few minutes early.

Using a glass door as a mirror, he straightened his tie and waited, expecting that, like most girls, Ellen would be a little late.

Sure enough the minutes passed, each one representing sixty seconds in which he could have been talking to Ellen, trying to get to know her in person rather than over the phone, trying to get her to like him as more than a voice.

Several times Alex thought he saw her turn the corner near the theater and each time his heart had palpitated until the disappointment of mistaken identity set in. The minutes continued to pass. Alex straightened his tie again. Soon he was less concerned with the conversation they might have and more worried that she might not show up at all.

At five minutes of two he went inside and asked the woman in the box office if anyone had left a message for Alex Lazar. The woman shook her head.

By two o'clock the crowd that had been standing outside the theater with Alex had all gone in. Alex now stood alone. Finally a taxicab pulled up. As Ellen got out the lights in the theater lobby blinked on and off. They rushed in and found their seats just as the curtain rose. Ellen quickly whispered an apology for being late. Then the audience grew quiet and the play began.

Alex's retention of the first act of the play was nil. Instead he spent most of it sneaking glances at Ellen. She looked just as pretty as the first time he'd seen her. Now, seated beside him, she made him feel both thrilled and anxious. Surely a girl who looked like that had been on many dates with many guys.

The intermission lights went on and Ellen turned to him. "Do you like it?"

"Yes," he lied.

"I think Florence Rodgers is just superb," she said.

Alex nodded, wondering who the hell Florence Rodgers was.

Then Ellen excused herself and went to the ladies' room. Alex looked up Florence Rodgers in the *Playbill*. She was the director. Up to that point in his life, Alex had hardly paid any attention to who directed plays and movies. But he knew Woody Allen wrote and directed his own movies, and since Ellen seemed interested in directors he figured he ought to think of something to say about Woody Allen.

He had plenty of time. Ellen spent almost the entire intermission in the ladies' room.

The second act seemed to be a repeat of the first. This time Alex tried to concentrate on the play, which was about a bunch of people who talked about death. Somehow he had difficulty relating to it.

Then the play was over and he and Ellen were standing outside the theater. For the first time he felt like they were together and could talk without distractions. Of course, the sidewalk in front of the theater wasn't exactly the best place.

"I thought it slowed up during the second act," Ellen said.

Alex agreed. Actually, as far as he was concerned, it had never gotten going. "Can I take you to dinner?" he asked.

Ellen smiled. "That's sweet, Alex, but I've already made plans."

"Oh." Alex scraped his shoe on the sidewalk. It occurred to him that she might be planning to leave momentarily. "Well," he said, feeling dejected, "let's try to get together again."

The next thing he knew Ellen slipped her arm through his. "I still have some time," she said. "Let's take a walk."

Arm in arm they walked through Times Square and across

42nd Street. They talked about Woody Allen and it turned out they were both big fans of his. Almost an hour passed while they reminded each other of the funniest scenes from their favorite Allen movies—the time in *Love and Death* when the crazy uncle displays the small plot of land he carries in his pocket, and the scene in *Bananas* when Allen buys thousands of deli sandwiches for the band of revolutionaries in the hills. And they laughed. They were walking through one of the raunchiest parts of town and as far as Alex was concerned he was in paradise.

Then he saw a street sign that said 24th Street. "I hope your dinner date's downtown," he said. The words were hardly out of his mouth when he began to regret them. Ellen looked up at the sign and then quickly at her watch.

"I'm supposed to be at Madison and Ninety-fourth Street in ten minutes," she gasped. Apparently it was more important that she be on time for her next date than it was for her date with Alex because she hurriedly began looking for a cab.

While Ellen stood in the street near the corner waving at cabs, Alex tried to bring a formal conclusion to what he felt was the premature end of their date. He thanked her for taking him to the play and again suggested they have another date sometime soon. A block away they both saw a yellow cab with its vacant light on. Ellen waved vigorously.

"I'm going to Europe over Christmas," she said as the cab pulled up. "I won't be back until after New Year's." She pulled open the door. "Call me then." The door slammed shut.

Driving home from the city Alex didn't know whether to be elated or miserable. On one hand he and Ellen had had a good time together, especially during their walk after the play. But on the other hand he felt like he was just one of who-knew-how-many guys she might have seen that day.

He chuckled sourly at the thought of her not having time for him again until after New Year's. He might have been crazy about her, but he wasn't crazed enough to believe there was a future in being squeezed here and there into Ellen's busy schedule. Or would she make more time for him? He'd just have to wait and see.

TEN

The drug business flourished. Alex and Michael sold the kilo in less than a month. Some of the kids bought ounces for themselves and their friends. Others bought three or four ounces, divided them into smaller lots and sold the grass to the sophomores and freshmen.

Alex was not surprised that the kilo went so fast. He had first smoked grass in the eighth grade and by his freshman year pot was as much a part of the high school life as intramural sports. For his entire high school career the smell of marijuana smoke in the bathroom and behind the utility garage was as common as the smell of musk on girls. Not everyone at school smoked grass, and among those who did, heavy users were in the minority. But most of the kids got high once in a while. As soon as the word got around that Alex was selling super grass at reasonable prices, few kids looked elsewhere for it.

They bought another kilo after Thanksgiving and two more just after New Year's. Alex couldn't believe how simple and apparently foolproof the arrangement was. They were paying about twenty dollars an ounce, which sold for forty. The kids seemed to think it was a bargain. He and Michael only sold to kids from school, kids who couldn't possibly be cops.

Alex, who got forty-dollars-a-week allowance and had charge cards for his gasoline and clothes, couldn't figure out what to do with all the money he was making. Most of it just sat, hidden in the back of his closet, wadded tightly with rubber bands. Once in a while he would take it out and stare at it in wonderment. Having come to him so easily, it didn't seem like real money at all.

By January Alex had actually gotten to the point where he preferred to give away small amounts of grass rather than deal. He simply didn't need the money and he was beginning to get a new kick from the grass—status. It was like being the goddamn Godfather. People liked to be seen walking with him in the halls, he was invited to just about every party and activity where drugs were consumed. In short, he was the primo dealer at Deepbrook High.

The only problem was Michael. As Alex had more fun in his role as dealer, Michael seemed to get meaner and nastier. Lately, no matter how much grass they sold, Michael never had any money and often got irritated when he heard that Alex had given grass away free. He looked pale and skinny. Alex knew Michael sometimes took pills, but when he tried to talk about it Michael wouldn't listen or would get antagonistic. Several times Michael had berated him in front of other kids for giving away grass and once he even called Alex "a rich punk," which almost earned him a punch in the mouth.

Michael seemed to have this idea that Alex was among the chosen few while he, Michael, was not. It was true that the kids

54

who went to Deepbrook High came from well-to-do communities. Not all of them were as exclusive as Upper Deepbrook, where Alex and his absentee parents lived, but most were pretty nice places. The kids got big allowances, they had charge cards, and if they didn't have cars of their own, they had frequent use of one of their parents' cars. There were a couple of kids, like Michael, who lived in what was considered the poorer part of Deepbrook, but to Alex even their plight seemed relative. To be considered poor in Deepbrook meant sharing a two-family house, owning only one car, and having one of those rubber pools in the backyard instead of a concrete job sunk in the earth.

The only time Alex and Michael spent together anymore was the time it took to buy kilos. Michael wasn't around Deepbrook as much. Instead he said he was hanging out at Chicken's place in Brooklyn, smoking grass and listening to reggae. And Michael talked about other drugs now, bragging about using cocaine and Quaaludes and, the one he mentioned most often, angel dust.

Chicken didn't have angel dust, but a friend of his did. Chicken would call him and Michael and Alex would go.

They could buy an ounce for $400 and mix it into a kilo of grass. Ounces of "dusted" grass sold for close to $80, so on an investment of $1,100 they could expect a return of $2,800.

Alex was not enthusiastic. Michael's preoccupation with maximum profits from minimum investment reminded him of his father. Besides, Michael was in bad shape. Whenever Alex saw him now he was either so zonked he could hardly talk or he was irritable and fidgety and quick to anger. Alex had originally said he didn't want to get involved with angel dust, which he'd heard was dangerous. But Michael had first argued with him and then practically begged him to do the dust deal. Michael said he needed the money and accused Alex of not understanding anything about money because his parents were rich. Alex asked him where all the money from the previous kilos had gone. Michael said he'd bought an expensive stereo system and was paying it off and hoped to put a down payment on a car. Alex was pretty sure Michael was lying, but he wondered if the kid was right about the money anyway. Alex's expensive stereo system had been a sixteenth-birthday present and the BMW had come the same way exactly one year later. Feeling guilty, Alex agreed to do the deal.

It was a bitter cold afternoon in January and they were driving around a part of Harlem that looked like a war had been fought in it. All they saw were empty, gutted buildings and lots filled with garbage and debris. There was no one on the sidewalk, hardly any cars on the street, and Alex wondered if anyone lived there at all. The place they were to meet Chicken's friend was an abandoned building like all the rest. Michael said the contact would be waiting for him inside.

Because Michael had said he was broke, Alex had to put up the four hundred dollars for the ounce of angel dust. They both got out of the car. It was so cold Alex zipped his jacket up to the neck.

"He ain't gonna dig you showin' up with me," Michael said, already shivering in his T-shirt and denim jacket. "Chicken told me to go alone."

"I don't like that idea," Alex said. "It's too easy for them to rip you off."

"I can handle it," Michael said, trying to sound tough.

Alex sighed. For someone who had grown so thin, Michael

was crazy to think he could scare away a determined robber with a mere sneer. "Michael, seriously, what if he's got some friends?"

"Then I've got this." Michael reached into his jeans and drew out a small black revolver. He stared at Alex with a cockeyed ferocity, holding the gun over the hood of the car so Alex could see it clearly.

"Jesus, Michael!" Alex jumped back a step and quickly looked around to see if anyone had seen Michael take the gun out. "Put it away, you've made your point."

"I told you, no one's gonna mess with me," Michael said ominously, slipping the gun back into his pants.

Alex couldn't believe Michael actually had a gun. Of all the stupid things . . . "Is it real?"

Michael frowned and reached toward his pants again.

"No, no, don't," Alex said. Michael was unpredictable enough without a gun. "Where'd you get it?"

"Chicken sold it to me for seventy-five dollars."

"Do you know how to use it?" Alex had never fired a gun in his life. He'd always assumed that they were fairly complicated to use and that maniacs like Michael couldn't just buy one and start shooting.

"You just squeeze the trigger, dummy," Michael said. "I killed a squirrel with it."

That was Michael, all right, trying out his new toy by murdering small defenseless animals. It was the same old game of Dare. Only this time it was with a gun instead of a stiletto. Alex stared at the living version of Billy the Kid across the car from him. Harlem, guns, and angel dust, he thought. Perhaps they had gone too far. "Michael, why don't you put the gun in the trunk and let's go home," Alex said. "I'm just not up for this stuff today. We don't even know what the guy we're supposed to buy from looks like."

"Chickenshit." Michael sneered, turned and went into the building.

Alex got back into the car and waited. Until recently Michael's tough guy act had amused Alex more than annoyed him. But now Alex was growing tired of both the act and Michael, who seemed to be getting crazier by the day. In fact, Alex was getting tired of the whole drug dealing scene. The other side of his status as primo dealer was the growing expectation among kids that he could and would supply everyone with everything. At parties he was treated like a walking drug dispensary and Alex was beginning to see that his recent popularity was predicated more on his reputation as a dealer than on his personal merits.

Michael returned to the car.

"You got it?" Alex asked.

"It's coming," Michael said.

"It's coming?"

"Yeah." Michael lit a cigarette.

Alex had a dreadful thought. "Michael, did you give someone my four hundred and not get any angel dust?"

"I told you, dummy, it's coming."

Had Michael fallen for the oldest trick in the con artist's book? Whoever took the four hundred was likely to disappear, not return. Alex tried to stay calm, tried to give Michael the benefit of whatever doubt or explanation could be mustered in such an idiotic situation. "What makes you think anyone is going to return with the dust?" he asked.

"I told him Chicken sent me." Michael apparently refused to believe that he could be duped so easily.

"Told who?"

"The kid," Michael said irritably.

"What kid?" Alex asked irritably.

"The kid I gave the money to," said Michael, turning to Alex. "Get off my case, man, I know what the fuck I'm doing."

Alex tried to stay quiet and wait, but even if the kid did come through, it was a ridiculous risk to take. He was so pissed at Michael. Four hundred dollars!

A few minutes passed. Michael was chain smoking and Alex had to open the car window to get some fresh air. Michael had a habit of flicking his ashes on the car floor and usually Alex tolerated it, but today it just added to his annoyance.

"Could you please not flick ashes all over the floor?" he said.

"*Could you please not flick ashes all over the floor?*" Michael mimicked him in a high, effeminate voice. To add to the insult he purposely flicked a particularly long ash. A violent feeling swept through Alex as he watched the ash fall to the floor mat in a gray heap. He really felt like pulverizing Michael. Didn't the kid have enough brains to know that you didn't give away four hundred dollars of someone else's money and then flick ashes all over his car? Never in his life had he known someone who could be so belligerent, so disagreeable, so needlessly negative.

Alex reached for the door handle and pushed the door open.

"Where are you going?" Michael asked.

"In there to see if I can get my money back," Alex said. He was scared to go in, but he wanted the money and he also wanted to get rid of Michael.

"You can't go in there," Michael said, following Alex out of the car.

"Just shut up, Michael, will you." Alex climbed the steps.

59

The windows of the building were boarded up. There was no front door, just a gaping doorway. It looked like no one had lived there for years. Inside, Alex knocked on the apartment door. No answer. He knocked again.

"I told you he's out getting the stuff," said Michael, who had followed Alex into the building.

Alex tried pushing the door.

"He's not gonna like that," Michael said.

Almost to spite Michael, Alex pushed harder on the door. It opened a few inches and Alex peeked inside. A single light bulb burned in the hallway, revealing a barren interior. There was no furniture, no carpeting, nothing hanging on the walls. Empty beer bottles, cigarette butts and old magazines littered the floor. No one lived there. Alex pushed the door open farther and stepped in carefully. A room to his right was nothing but the same: junk all over the floor.

Something crashed behind him and Alex jumped around half expecting to find a gang of muggers. Instead he found Michael on his knees.

"Fuckin' bottle," Michael mumbled. On the floor behind Michael Alex saw the beer bottle he'd slipped on. He also saw Michael's gun, which had apparently fallen out of his pants. Alex bent down and picked it up. It was pretty heavy for such a little thing.

"Hey, gimme that," Michael said as he got up.

But Alex held it a moment longer. It reminded him of the toy guns he'd played with as a kid. Only there'd been toy bullets in the toy barrel.

"There are no bullets," Alex said, handing the gun back to Michael, who quickly stuck it back in his pants.

"I used 'em up," Michael said.

"So what good is carrying the gun?" Alex asked.

"Hey, man, I'm gonna get bullets," Michael said. "I just gotta find some."

"Find some?"

"You know, find a place where they sell 'em."

Despite everything that had happened that afternoon, Alex started to laugh. He couldn't help it. Michael had a gun, but didn't know where to get bullets. This was the best bluff yet.

A door opened and slammed.

"That's him," Michael said. "See, I told you."

A black kid several years younger than Alex came toward them. He couldn't have weighed more than a hundred and twenty pounds. When he saw Alex he frowned.

"Your friend?" he said to Michael.

"He's a friend of Chicken's," Michael said.

"Yeah, Chicken," the kid snorted. He found something about the name amusing but didn't explain what.

"My friend didn't think you'd come back," Michael said, "but I knew you would."

Alex felt embarassed. "Well," he said, trying to explain, "I just didn't know and it was a lot of money."

The kid ignored him. From his pocket he took a package of tin foil and opened it carefully. Inside was the angel dust, a dull white powder with many small transparent crystals that reflected the light from the light bulb above them. The kid again reached into his pants, this time taking out a long black switchblade. It looked too large for his small hand as he flicked it open and dipped the point into the powder and held it up to Michael. "Try some," he said.

Holding one nostril closed, Michael leaned over the point of the knife and inhaled. He straightened up, holding his nose.

Alex watched a tear form in his friend's eye, but Michael quickly wiped it away.

The kid dipped the point of the knife in again and this time offered it to Alex, but he declined. "He'll tell me," Alex said, nodding toward Michael.

"It's good," Michael said.

The kid nodded, handed the open package to Alex and dipped the knife point in once again, this time removing a heap of powder which he dropped into a plastic pill container of his own. "My tip," he said.

Going back to the car Michael was, to say the least, in high spirits. He wasn't quite walking; it was more of a wobble. When he reached the BMW he just stood and stared helplessly at the door.

"Get in, Michael," Alex said.

Michael grinned and his eyes sort of rolled around. "Door won't open," he said in slow, lethargic words that seemed to drool out of his mouth.

"Door won't open until Michael pulls handle," Alex said.

But Michael just stood at the door, waiting. It was so cold Alex thought his ears were going to solidify right on his head, so he got in the car, reached across the seat and opened the door for Michael. Michael got in slowly and turned to Alex. His eyes had a dull matte finish. "See?"

"See what?" Alex started the car.

"Door open."

Alex knew Michael's body was in the car, but he suspected his friend's mind was hovering somewhere over Nova Scotia. "Michael, close door," he said.

But Michael only stared at the door while a frigid gust of air blew in. Alex reached across Michael and pulled the door closed. Michael turned toward Alex again. "See?"

"See what?"

"Door close," Michael said triumphantly.

Alex pointed down to the floor of the car where some of the cigarette ashes from Michael's cigarettes still lay. "See?"

Michael leaned over and stared at the floor. "See what?"

"Michael's brain," Alex said.

For the drive home Michael was a one-man stoned slapstick comedy. First, he tried to light three cigarettes at once. Alex smelled something odd and looking over he saw that Michael was lighting more hair than cigarette. He calmly removed the matches from Michael's grip. Next, Michael wanted to play with his gun, and a monosyllabic debate ensued. It went like this: "Yes," "No," "Yes," "No," "Yes," "No," etc, until Michael forgot what the debate was about. Then at sixty miles per hour, Michael yanked on the door handle. Alex was prepared for this and quickly reached across and pulled the door closed. Michael even drooled and Alex wiped his lower lip with a tissue. He wasn't sure, but he suspected Michael purposely did it just to see what he would do.

As they approached Deepbrook Michael began to come down. It was a bumpy descent. Making his first coherent sentence in an hour, Michael said, "Don't take me home."

Alex drove past Michael's house. "Where do you want to go?"

Michael didn't answer for a while and Alex cruised through town thinking about the angel dust in the car. Finally, Michael said he wanted to go to the train station.

"Mind if I ask why?"

"I'm goin' to the city," Michael said, biting his nails.

"We just came from there."

"I'm goin' to Chicken's," Michael said.

"You want to go to my house?" Alex asked. Normally he didn't invite Michael over because Lucille hated him, but Michael was acting weird and Alex wasn't sure the drug had worn off completely.

"Take me to the train station," Michael insisted. There was a nervous, almost hysterical timbre in his voice. Alex was reluctant to let him go to the city like that.

"I want to go to the train station," Michael said loudly. Was it anger or panic? Alex wondered.

At the station Michael wanted some of the angel dust. When Alex reminded him that they usually divided their purchases up evenly before dipping into the stash, Michael practically had a fit, alternating between threats and pleas and all the while cursing. He seemed almost irrational.

"Gimme my half," he said.

"Technically you don't own a half," Alex said. "I paid for all of it."

"You're a thief," Michael yelled.

The old anger from that afternoon welled up in Alex. *So belligerent, so disagreeable.*

"A fucking thief."

Suddenly Alex twisted around and punched Michael as hard as he could in the arm.

"Ow!" Michael rebounded off the door. "You . . ." Alex raised his fist again and Michael didn't finish the sentence. Shaking a little from anger and surprise at what he'd done, Alex took out the angel dust and poured some into the cellophane from a pack of cigarettes. Michael watched quietly, looking like he was going to cry. Alex handed the cellophane to him and Michael got out and slammed the door. Outside Michael turned and yelled something at him, but Alex couldn't hear it over the roar of the car engine as he sped away.

ELEVEN

At home Alex stashed the dust in his room and went downstairs to see what Lucille had prepared for dinner. He found her watching television in the kitchen. Where there was usually a place set for his dinner, tonight the table was bare.

"Alexander, where you been all day?" the small black woman asked.

"Out." He sat down at the table, took a cigarette out of his pocket and lit it with his lighter, El Zippo.

Lucille frowned. "You know I don't like smokin' in the kitchen. That smell gets into everything."

"I'll only smoke half."

Lucille would usually laugh when he said something like that. Tonight her face remained impassive.

"What's for dinner?" he asked.

"Grill's closed for the night," Lucille said. "You forgot to call and say if you'd be home to eat."

"You could heat something up. It wouldn't be a big deal." As a conciliatory gesture, he crushed out the cigarette.

"Suppose I could, child. But exactly where were you today?"

It pissed Alex off when she got nosy like that. Lately she questioned him almost every time he came home. "That's my business, Lucille."

"Your business is my business," Lucille said sharply. "There's no one else in this house to watch out for you. You were out with that no good Michael Martin smokin' reefer, weren't you?"

"So what if I was?" Alex said. "Even you said there's nothing wrong with a little grass now and then."

"No, there ain't," Lucille said. "But there's something wrong with Michael Martin and there's something wrong with these all-day disappearin' acts of yours. And how come you keep goin' out late at night after school and comin' back twenty minutes later? You think I don't know what you're up to? There are only two reasons why a boy would be sneakin' out that late and excuse me for sayin' so, but I don't know any girls in this neighborhood who are *that* fast."

Alex sighed and didn't say anything.

Lucille stared at him, her lips pressed tightly together. "Used to be," she said, "when I grew up my brothers were always goin' out to the midnight auto supply when they needed a part for their cars. It was the only store in the county opened all night, 'cept it wasn't listed no where, no address, nothin'." She shook her head and went to the refrigerator to get some dinner for Alex. "Never thought I'd see the day when Alexander Lazar would be runnin' the midnight drugstore."

TWELVE

Before his first class on Monday, Alex looked for James in the school cafeteria, but there was no sign of the noble gnome. Snow was falling fast and heavily outside so Alex knew James wasn't having a smoke behind the utility garage.

He was just about to go to the library when he noticed a solitary figure trudging through the snow outside the cafeteria window. It wasn't so much a person as a large green coat with a fur-lined hood. In the blowing snow it could have been mistaken for an evergreen bush, except that it moved slowly toward the door.

Alex waited in the vestibule for the coat to arrive.

"Are you in there, James?" he asked as the coat stepped slowly inside.

"There is little justice in this world and even less sympathy on the part of certain bus drivers," the coat replied, its teeth chattering.

"Miss the bus?"

James shook the snow off. "Because of this gargantuan coat. I was half a block from the bus stop when the bus arrived, but I kept tripping on the bottom of the coat. Just as I got there the bus driver pulled away."

"I don't blame him," Alex laughed. "If I saw you coming in that thing I'd pull away also. Where'd you get it?"

"It's my brother Eddie's. An authentic Vietnam airman's coat. I wear it in penance for our sins abroad." James pulled the hood back and shook the snow off. Small drifts formed on the floor beneath it.

Underneath James was wearing his normal outfit: a wrinkled blue shirt, a pair of ancient khaki pants with cuffs, and his favorite footwear, purple basketball sneakers with more holes in them than Swiss cheese.

"I feel I need a cigarette," James said as he stuffed the coat into his locker. "Come, let us retire to the men's lounge."

In the boys' room Alex took out a joint and whispered, "Rolled with angel dust."

"Angel dust?" James looked surprised.

"You want to try it?" Alex asked.

"I dunno," James said. "We've got Mormon's class the period after next."

Alex explained that the high didn't last that long. James was persuaded.

Alex took the joint first and went down to the last stall while James lingered at a urinal near the entrance to the boys' room. "Remember," James said, "one flush means you're safe, two flushes means danger."

In the last stall Alex lit the joint and inhaled. It tasted funny, sort of metallic. Several tokes later, Alex stepped out of the stall unsteadily. The bathroom felt like it was rocking back and forth and when he closed his eyes he felt like he was on a ship.

Walking toward James he had to keep one hand on the wall for balance.

He gave the joint to James. "Just take a couple of tokes," he said. "That's all you need."

James went into the stall and Alex took up guard duty by the first urinal. He felt like he was underwater. Every straight line seemed to bend and every sound was slushy. Alex imagined that amoebas always felt like this.

He heard the bathroom door open and caught his breath. A second later Principal Seekamp strolled in and Alex hit the flusher twice. The corresponding flush sounded in the last stall as James dispatched the joint into the bowels of the school's plumbing system.

Seekamp stared at Alex, scowled and sniffed the air. When the principal turned toward the last stall Alex started whistling. Just as Seekamp arrived at the stall, James popped out grinning. But the principal walked right past him and looked into the stall.

James bit his lip.

"Have a good crap, Lasky?" Seekamp asked.

"Uh, yes, sir."

The principal stepped out of the stall and looked down at James. "Always good to get a load off your mind before a hard day at school, huh?"

"Yes, it is," James said, teetering slightly and holding onto the stall wall for balance.

Seekamp watched him. "Tell me, Lasky, when was the last time you changed your underwear?"

"Uh, this morning."

"And when do you plan to change them again?"

"Tonight."

70

"That's good, Lasky. You know why?" Seekamp asked with a malicious look.

"No, sir."

"Because there's no toilet paper in that stall, Lasky."

Alex cracked up.

"You'd think by now someone would have toilet-trained you, Lasky." Seekamp continued dressing James down. "Think we ought to speak to the school nurse about this. What do you say we take a little trip down to see Miss Lewis, huh, Lasky? And maybe we ought to stop in to see the school psychologist, too. I imagine there must be some other maladjustments in there."

"No, sir. I really don't think that's necessary," James said.

"What do you mean, not necessary?" Seekamp asked. He was having a fine time. "You're not trying to tell me that you weren't taking a crap, are you?"

"Uh, no, sir."

Seekamp sniffed again. "You're sure now, Lasky. It does smell a bit peculiar in here. What does it smell like to you?"

James pretended to sniff the air, which was pungent with marijuana smoke. "I don't smell anything."

"You sure?"

"Sure, I'm sure, sure. I mean sir," James said. The bell to change classes rang and kids began to come into the bathroom. Most of them stopped near Alex when they saw Seekamp and James at the other end of the room.

"Well, are you going to promise to wipe next time?" Seekamp asked.

James glanced at the spectators and nodded quickly.

"I didn't hear you, Lasky. What did you say?"

"I'll wipe next time," James whispered, growing red.

"What?" Seekamp barked.

71

"I'll wipe next time," James said a decibel louder.

"Christ, Lasky, I think I'll have to make you write that on a blackboard a hundred times because I can't hear you," Seekamp prodded.

"I'LL WIPE NEXT TIME!" James yelled. Alex was startled. Even Seekamp jumped. James stood with his fists clenched, fuming.

"Glad to hear it, Lasky." Seekamp nodded and walked out of the bathroom.

"Philistine," James muttered.

Somehow they made it to the library. The hallways were particularly treacherous because the floors felt mushy, and James and Alex kept imagining that they were sinking in the tiles. The end of the hallway appeared to wag as if the boys were walking down a huge dog's tail.

"Note how the end of the hallway appears to wag as if we're walking down a huge dog's tail," James said.

They picked a table in the far corner where they were least likely to disturb the students who actually used the library for study purposes. James fixed his attention on the table where the girl from Florida sat.

"Still haven't introduced yourself?" Alex asked in the same slow-motion speech Michael had used a few days before.

"Don't rush me," James said. "There are multifarious factors to consider."

"Genes?"

"Questions of propriety," said James, shaking his head as if he were trying to wake up. "I feel like an amoeba in need of a good night's sleep."

"That makes three of us," Alex said.

72

The bell rang and they got up slowly, the influence of the angel dust still upon them. Alex wondered how they would fare in their next class—English, with Miss Mormon.

Miss Mormon stood over six feet tall, was built like a Mack truck, had a face that resembled a cinder block, and was strong enough to crush chalk in her bare hands. Her reputation for cruelty to students was so bad that kids who didn't even go to Deepbrook feared her.

James and Alex got to class early and took their seats together in the back of the room. James, hunched over his desk, started tracing a circle around and around on a piece of paper. He was, to use one of his own terms, chemically debilitated. Alex looked at the students around them, chatting among themselves, unaware of the two stoned creatures in the back of the class. For how long? he wondered.

Then Miss Mormon stomped into the room, leaving a wake of silence behind her. She looked about two feet larger than normal in every direction and snakes were crawling around her head. They were supposed to be studying *Julius Caesar* and Alex realized he'd forgotten to go back to his locker to get his copy of Shakespeare.

"James," he whispered.

"Not here," the gnome whispered back.

"James, I forgot my book."

James slipped a book on his desk, but when Alex opened it, he found graphs and equations. Miss Mormon was asking for volunteers to read the play. Alex turned to another part of the book: more equations. James had given him a geometry text. Alex looked to James for help, but the gnome had gone back to tracing the circle.

Sometime later in the class, Alex thought he heard Miss

73

Mormon say, "Mr. Lazar, are you prepared to read?"

Green kernels of popcorn started popping in his mind. He didn't have the right book. He couldn't have read out loud even if he had. In fact, he wasn't even sure he could stand up and answer Miss Mormon coherently.

Across the room Monster Mormon waited for his reply. A dark cloud of doom began to thicken over Alex.

"May I read, Miss Mormon?" The voice had come from Alex's right, from James. The class churned with whispers and the scraping of chair legs as stunned students turned to look. No one could remember James Lasky volunteering for anything.

"Class!" The walls shook with Miss Mormon's voice.

James's bait had been strong enough to pull her away from Alex, who was, so to speak, off the hook.

Now the monster savored her new worm. "Mr. Lasky, I am delighted," she said in a particularly sinister tone. "Is there a part you wish to recite?"

James sat in silence for a moment. As far as Alex knew, James hadn't even read the play yet. James was the kind of student who didn't open a book until the night before an exam, but rarely got less than an A. Alex watched as his friend and savior scratched his head and said, "How about the chariot scene?"

The class disintegrated into laughter, and Miss Mormon's face grew long and red. A piece of chalk in her left hand turned into powder and a row of stainless-steel teeth glinted through her snarling lips. She reached for a yardstick and smashed it against the desk with a loud crack. The class went silent. Like Godzilla ravaging Tokyo, Miss Mormon marched through the

74

rows of desks. She stopped at Alex and stared at the geometry book. "Where is your Shakespeare, Mr. Lazar?"

Alex cowered and shrugged.

Miss Mormon turned to James and picked up the piece of paper. James had traced the circle so many times that it fell out when she lifted it.

"Is this what you did all period, Mr. Lasky?"

James nodded blankly.

"Both of you, to the principal's office at once," she said and marched down the hall behind them.

Seekamp was on the phone when they arrived. He put his hand over the mouthpiece when they entered. "What are the charges, Miss Mormon?" he asked solemnly. Alex's eyes felt as if they were rolling around loosely in his head.

"I would like to know why Mr. Lasky spent the entire period doing this." She held up the piece of paper, *avec* hole.

"And Lazar?" the principal asked.

"Came to class unprepared," Miss Mormon said. "I expect harsh discipline." She left the office.

James and Alex sat down and waited for Seekamp to finish his conversation.

Seekamp hung up. "Christ, didn't I just see you two an hour ago?"

Alex and James nodded and Seekamp scratched his jaw. "Okay, Lasky, what's the story?"

"I volunteered to recite the chariot scene in *Julius Caesar*," James said innocently.

"What's wrong with that?" Seekamp asked.

"There is no chariot scene in *Julius Caesar*," James explained. "I got it mixed up with *Ben Hur*."

Seekamp nodded. "I liked *Ben Hur* more myself." Then he turned to Alex. "What about you, Lazar?"

"I liked *Ben Hur* more," Alex said.

"No, no." Seekamp shook his head. "I meant, why were you unprepared for class?"

"I forgot my book," Alex said.

Seekamp picked up the piece of paper. "What about this?"

"I drew a circle on that piece of paper," James answered with a straight face.

Seekamp looked at the piece of paper and then at James and Alex. "Okay." He smirked. "I know these are difficult times for you young studs and you like to blow off steam by goofing up in class, but I'm tired of seeing you here, especially you, Lasky. This is the second time this morning. You guys know Miss Mormon gets a little sensitive, but she's a damn good teacher, and if you had half a brain collectively you'd learn from her instead of hassling her. Now you've got four months left here and if you can't behave, just stay out of her way and then you'll get out of here and never see her or me again. And frankly, we'd like that just as much as you, understand?"

They nodded in unison. Alex considered saluting.

"Otherwise, you're gonna spend the next four months washing blackboards. Got that?"

Again they nodded.

"Okay." Seekamp smiled. "Now beat it."

They did.

THIRTEEN

Lucille managed to serve dinner that night without adding a lecture to the main course. The phone rang just as Alex sat down at the dinner table. Lucille answered it.

"Who is it, Lucille?" Alex asked as he cut into his veal parmesan, his favorite food.

Lucille put her hand over the receiver. "A girl," she said. "Should I tell her to call back after dinner?"

Alex nodded. He had just put the first piece of veal in his mouth when he heard Lucille say "Ellen" and start to hang up.

"Wait!" He jumped up and grabbed the phone, but it was too late, Ellen had hung up. Lucille watched skeptically as he dialed her number. Ellen answered.

"Hi, how are you?" he said.

"Fine," Ellen replied. "That woman told me you were eating."

"Uh, well I was, but I finished."

"She said you just sat down."

"It was one of your faster meals," Alex said and looked at

Lucille, who was watching and listening. She pointed to the veal and mouthed the words, "It will get cold." Nothing got Lucille angrier than when Alex let his dinners get cold. Alex nodded, but didn't get off the phone. He asked Ellen how her trip had been and she told him about the skiing conditions in Europe. Meanwhile Lucille kept giving him the angry eye.

After she finished telling him about Europe, Ellen asked if he'd like to come to her house that Saturday. "It's Exit Forty-six on the Sunshine Parkway," she said. "Follow the road all the way to the water."

"Uh, fine, sure, okay." Alex felt somewhere between ecstasy and disbelief.

"Is something not okay?" Ellen asked.

Tripping over his thoughts, Alex stammered, "Well, I guess I just expected it to be a little harder, I mean I didn't expect you to call, I mean I'm glad you did, I don't mind, but . . ."

"Oh," Ellen said. "Shall I play harder to get? Fine, let's move the date back one year. You can visit me at college."

"No, no. Really, I'll see you on Saturday."

"Okay, bye."

Alex put the receiver back on the hook and stared at it. Was that really Ellen? Had she really invited him out for the day?

"Boy, I never thought I'd see the day when some girl would wrap you around her little finger," Lucille said.

Alex clutched his heart dramatically. "Lucille," he shouted, "I'm in love . . . practically!"

FOURTEEN

Before going to Southampton Saturday morning, Alex drove to Deepbrook to have the BMW washed. *That* was an indication of his seriousness about Ellen, he thought. Never before had he gone so far to make a good impression.

Driving into town he passed Michael's house. Michael hadn't been around all week. On Monday James said he'd seen some men in dark coats in Seekamp's office. "They looked like narcs," James had said.

When Michael didn't show up at the utility garage on Tuesday or Wednesday, Alex began to worry. If Michael had been busted, he'd be next.

Wednesday night he put the angel dust and every bit of grass he could find in a jar and put that jar in a larger jar and buried it in his backyard. Each morning he went to the school library and read the local newspapers, looking for news about Michael. James saw him there so much he asked Alex if he were trying to muscle in on his Florida dream girl.

Alex began to see, or imagined he saw, dark unmarked sedans following him wherever he drove. Each morning he drove to school through the rear entrance and checked to see if any police cars were parked in front. On Thursday afternoon he passed Seekamp in the hall and the principal nodded at him, but said nothing. What did that nod mean? Alex wondered. Did it just mean hello? Did it mean, sorry about Michael? Could it have meant, you're next? That night Alex dug up the jar and reburied it in a more remote place.

On Friday night Alex dreamed that a bunch of policemen rushed into Monster Mormon's class in the middle of his perfect recitation of Anthony's funeral oration and, ignoring his pleas to let him finish, dragged him away.

But now it was Saturday morning and the police had still not come for him. The sun was breaking through the clouds out over the Atlantic as he turned off Sea Spray Drive and drove up the long white pebble driveway to a big stucco house sharing a common courtyard with some smaller buildings. Alex parked his car in the courtyard.

The main house looked like a château with tall French windows on the second floor, each with its own balcony. One of the carved wood doors opened and Ellen, wearing blue jeans and a navy turtleneck sweater, walked toward him.

"Did you have any trouble getting here?" she asked.

"No." He'd actually forgotten again how pretty she was and now seeing her made him feel nervous. His natural reaction in such situations was to pretend not to notice. So he looked past her and through a space between two of the buildings. He could see the Atlantic, deep blue-green waves curling up and crashing down on the beach behind the house. "It's pretty here," he said, thinking how pretty she was.

"Yes." She smiled awkwardly and he wondered if she was embarrassed by her castle by the sea.

"I love the ocean," he said, thinking he could fall in love with her.

"Oh, would you like to go down there?" she asked. "Why don't you come in while I get my coat."

Inside, he waited in a room with a big fireplace and wide windows that faced the sea. Standing near the windows was a sextant on a wooden pedestal, a huge old ship's compass, an astrolabe and a telescope. The room was lined wall to wall with books, many of them with German titles. There were also models of sailboats on the shelves. Alex thought Ellen's father would have been a little old for models, but you never knew.

Ellen returned wearing a long sheepskin coat, and took him out back and across the dunes to the beach. A cold wind blew spray off the water. Alex loved it there. When he was a little kid, his parents sometimes rented a house on Cape Cod in the summer and while they were off sailing with friends or going to cocktail parties he would sit on the beach and watch the waves. It was something he never tired of, something he never felt lonely doing even when he was alone.

They stood quietly for a while, listening to the waves. Ellen's cheeks and the tip of her nose were red from the cold wind and her hair was shining and blowing around. He cautioned himself not to rush anything with her. She was the first girl he'd met in a long time that made him feel that if he lost her it would be a long time before he met someone else as desirable.

"You know," he said, "I've been thinking about your having to get off the phone at eight o'clock. Is that for real?"

"Oh, it's not so bad," she laughed. "Poppa's just that way. He's very serious about our education. We can't watch television after eight either."

"A strict upbringing, huh?"

He must have sounded critical because she looked right into his eyes and said, "He's Austrian and it's part of his idea of how to raise us. We've really never had a mother so I guess he tends to be overprotective. He doesn't have many friends anymore and he spends a lot of time with us. We're very close."

"What happened to your mom?"

Her gaze dropped to the sand. "She died of cancer when Joyce was three." She looked up at him. "Don't say anything about it in front of Poppa."

"I wouldn't."

They walked down the beach and Ellen told him how her grandfather, Gunther Schapmann, Sr., came to America with nothing except the heritage of many generations of Viennese bakers and alone built G. Schapmann and Sons. Alex said he always saw Schapmann cakes and cookies in the food store and thought they were pretty good. Ellen seemed to appreciate the compliment.

They walked quite a way down the beach and when Alex looked back toward the Schapmann place, the buildings looked doll-sized. "I didn't see your father back at the house."

"He's down at the boat yard, working on our sloop," Ellen said. "We start working on it in January so that by March we can be sailing. You'll meet him at dinner."

"Does that mean I'm invited?"

"If you like."

"I like."

They walked farther down the beach until they came across a

cluttered pile of driftwood, strands of rope, and other refuse coughed up by the sea. Alex, an inveterate beachcomber in his youth, wanted to investigate, but Ellen caught his arm and held him back.

"Don't look."

"Why not?" He stopped and she let go of his arm.

"Didn't you see *Jaws*?"

He shook his head.

"It was about the south shore, right along here. The man who wrote it lives a town or two over. Everybody was so mad at him because he scared the tourists away."

"So?"

"There's a scene in the movie where they find a girl's arm in a clump of junk like that. The shark ate the rest of her."

"And you think there might be an arm in that clump?" He scowled.

"I get the creeps every time I see one," she said.

For her sake he acquiesced and they continued past the debris. "I saw a shark like that once," he said, sitting down on the sand. She sat next to him. "In fact, the captain of the boat I was on almost caught it."

"Really!?" Ellen got excited.

"It was about five years ago," Alex said. "My father and some of his friends rented a boat to go deep-sea fishing and they took me along. We got into a school of bluefish and everyone was catching them. Then, like magic, they all disappeared. We couldn't figure out why until this monster shark came up to the surface about twenty feet from the boat. It was the biggest thing I'd ever seen, and confident, too. It swam right up to us and nudged the boat with its nose. I swear its mouth was big enough to swallow me whole. And there I was, leaning way out over the gunwale to get a closer look."

Ellen put her hand over her mouth.

"My father held on to my pants," Alex added. "Anyway, the captain, he was some kind of shark hunter and got all excited and ran into the cabin and got a rod about as thick as a baseball bat with a reel like this." Alex held his hands out as if a basketball were between them. "Then he took a whole bluefish and hooked it to a hook about the size of a hammer and threw it overboard. The shark actually took it, too."

"Really?" Ellen's dark eyes were wide.

"Oh, yes," Alex nodded. So far the story had basically been true, but at this point Alex launched into fantasy. "The string on the reel was as thick as clothesline and as soon as the shark was hooked it peeled off like he'd hooked a submarine or something."

"What happened?" Ellen asked, nearly breathless.

"Well, the captain started to tighten the drag to slow the shark down, but instead the boat started to move. The shark was pulling it. The weird thing was, it was pulling us right back toward port. So instead of trying to reel in, the captain just tied the line to a cleat and let the shark pull us home."

Ellen now looked at Alex suspiciously.

Alex put his hand over his heart. "Boy Scout's honor," said he who had never been a Boy Scout. "It towed us all the way into port. The captain was so appreciative he cut the line and let it go."

Alex watched as the expression on Ellen's face went from surprise to disbelief to shock and finally to anger. He started to laugh.

"Oh, you're such a creep!" Ellen yelled, apparently not seeing the humor. She stood up and marched away toward the

84

house. Alex was laughing so hard he couldn't get up at first, but when the implications of Ellen's anger sank in, he quickly rose and ran until he caught up to her.

"It was only a joke," he panted.

"Some joke," she said, walking quickly and not looking at him.

"Really, I didn't mean to insult you or anything."

"Insult? Ha! It was cruel and insensitive as well as juvenile," she said coldly, now jogging.

Alex began to feel panicked. "I'm sorry, really." He had to jog to keep up with her.

"Of course you are." Despite her heavy coat she jogged quickly. "You've been here less than half an hour and already you've taken advantage of my trusting nature and innocence."

"Trusting nature and innocence?" Alex gasped, struggling to run in the sand.

"Never in my life have I been so humiliated."

"My God, I'm sorry, I didn't think you'd be so sensitive." Whatever hopes he'd had for them began to disappear like a balloon rising up out of sight in the sky.

Ellen's jog accelerated to a run, and Alex, who'd let himself get out of shape, was having a hard time keeping up with her on the sand. He wasn't having much luck trying to understand her either.

"I'm afraid you'll just have to go," Ellen said without breaking stride.

"Have to go?" Alex said between deep breaths. "But Ellen . . ." He couldn't keep up with her. How could this happen? he asked himself, slowing down and finally stopping to sit in the sand and catch his breath. Certainly she had to be a little strange to take it so seriously.

Alex looked up and saw Ellen standing about ten feet from him. She wasn't even breathing hard and had an amused look on her face. "You sure are out of shape," she said, now laughing herself.

Alex felt his face turning red. "Very funny, very, very funny." But he too had to laugh.

A few minutes later, after they'd recovered and started back toward the house, Alex held her hand.

Gunther Schapmann looked more like a garage mechanic than the owner of a large commercial bakery. When he came home, just before dinner, he was wearing gray overalls and a pair of goggles on his head. His face, except for a raccoonlike stripe across his eyes, was covered with a fine, rust-colored powder.

Ellen introduced Alex, and her father shook his hand without smiling and then excused himself, saying he had to change for dinner.

They sat at a long table in a large dimly lit dining room lined with old wooden cabinets. A cook paraded around lighting candles, filling crystal with water, and serving food. Gunther sat down, followed by Ellen on his right and Joyce, who had just arrived from a friend's house, on his left. Alex sat opposite Gunther.

Dinner was served, beginning with a cream of mushroom soup. But no one touched a spoon until Gunther did. The same occurred with the main course of breaded veal and potatoes. You didn't eat unless Gunther did; you didn't talk unless Gunther addressed you. They ate in silence. Alex was used to talking through meals. Food was something you were required to put in your mouth so that someone else got a turn to speak.

86

But the only words spoken during dinner were by Gunther to the cook. Ellen smiled reassuringly at Alex and Joyce glanced inquisitively at him. Chocolate cake was served for dessert and Gunther had coffee, but Alex and the girls were given tea.

Afterward Gunther leaned back in his chair and lit a long, foul-smelling cigar. Ellen had warned Alex earlier that the smell was nauseating, and she was right. Alex wondered if you had to ask Gunther for permission to puke.

Gunther blew a smoke ring toward the ceiling and watched it dissolve in the air. Ellen gazed at Alex and smiled. Joyce stared dreamily at a candle.

"So, Alex," Gunther Schapmann said, "Ellen has told me only that you are the son of Carla Lazar, our former county executive. She neglected to tell me how you met."

Alex nearly choked on an after-dinner pastry. After clearing his throat he bumbled through a very poor explanation, saying he'd gotten lost in Brooklyn looking for a shortcut to the city and had stopped at the bakery because he was hungry.

Gunther frowned slightly and looked at Ellen and then back at Alex. "Surely any shortcut to the city would be through Queens, not Brooklyn."

"Well, I was lost," Alex said sheepishly.

Gunther nodded. "Quite lost."

Alex nodded. "Yes, quite lost."

"Perhaps you would have been better off asking for directions instead of pastry," Gunther said.

Alex thought this was meant to be funny and laughed, more from nervousness than mirth. But no one else laughed and Alex quickly stopped. Joyce stared at him as if he were weird.

Gunther continued asking questions and Alex realized that he was undergoing an interrogation thinly disguised as after-dinner conversation. He explained how his mother had left her county executive job to run for Congress and had lost. Then he told them how his father's company, Razal (Lazar backward) Dazal Wallpaper, Inc., used to make the ugliest wallpaper he'd ever seen. Each design was made of shiny silver or gold foil in strange stripes or zigzag patterns. Both girls said they'd seen it. So had a lot of other people because Mr. Lazar had made it the third biggest wallpaper company in the country before a big conglomerate came along and gobbled it up.

That did two things to his father, Alex said: it made him a lot of money and it left him unemployed. Now he passed his time sailing, jogging, playing golf, betting on horses and jai alai, and advising his friends on how to sell their companies so that they could become wealthy unemployed people with nothing to do but play with him.

Gunther said he thought it was a bad idea for a man whose whole life had been business to retire so early. In a way Alex agreed. Then Ellen's father got up and shook Alex's hand, saying he was pleased to meet him.

Apparently Alex had passed the *Are-you-good-enough-for-my-daughter?* test.

Later that night, after Gunther and Joyce had gone to sleep, Alex and Ellen sat on a couch before a fire in the room by the sea and talked about the dinner conversation.

"You're not the first to be interrogated," she said, snuggling close to him.

"Why does he do it?"

"To make sure. I told you he's very protective."

"Doesn't it bother you?" Alex very uncarelessly let his arm fall across her shoulders.

"A little, but I knew you'd do well." She smiled warmly at him. "Were you really lost when you came into the bakery?"

"In a sense."

"Sounds mysterious."

"It was meant to," Alex said. "Anyway, what if I turned out to be the son of a garbage man?"

"Then Poppa would tell me that he disapproved."

"And you would go along with that?"

"I don't know, Alex. It would depend on how I felt about garbage men's handsome sons."

"Boy, it would piss me off if my father ever did that," Alex said.

"But he only does it because he loves me, Alex. You shouldn't think anything about it."

"Actually," Alex said, leaning closer to her, "I think I can find better things to think about." He kissed her on the lips.

She allowed him for a moment, but then gently pushed him away.

"You shouldn't have let me kiss you if you didn't want me to," Alex said, annoyed and a little worried that she hadn't liked the way he kissed her.

"I wanted you to," she said. "But I want to be more comfortable."

"Oh. Should I get you some pillows?"

She shook her head.

"A back rub?"

"No."

"Soft music?"

"Sorry."

"What would make you more comfortable?"

She stood up and pulled him by the hand. "Time," she said, leading him to the closet and giving him his jacket.

FIFTEEN

On Monday Seekamp summoned Alex to his office.

As Alex walked down the hall he assumed that the principal was going to talk either about his poor grades again or about what Alex planned to do next year. But when he arrived in the office and sat down, Seekamp had something a little more serious on his mind.

"Alex, I've heard some very disturbing news about you," he said. The usual jocular reprimanding tone was absent and there was nothing informal about the principal as he sat stiffly behind his desk. "I'm not going to accuse you of anything, but I think you know what I'm talking about."

Alex didn't say anything. Seekamp looked at him for a long, silent moment.

"Alex," the principal said, "no one can tell you what to do or not to do. I think it's fairly obvious to all of us that you're out to prove you're your own man. If you think you have to prove it by quitting the tennis team and doing poorly in school, that's your business. To be frank, we didn't really expect you to go to Wimbledon or Harvard. That's one of the pitfalls of growing up the way you and some of your friends have grown up. You never learn to work hard for anything."

Alex winced. Seekamp was calling him a spoiled brat.

"To be honest, Alex," Seekamp continued, "whether or not you play on the tennis team or get good grades isn't going to affect your future that much. Some kids need scholarships, you obviously don't. But if you get caught selling drugs, your future will go straight down the shit hole. You don't have any idea now how gravely it could affect your life, but you better listen, Alex. You will regret it. You really will."

Seekamp waited for a reply, but Alex was too shocked to give him one. He wasn't about to admit that he was dealing or promise that he wouldn't do it anymore, nor did it seem wise to deny what Seekamp thought was so obvious. For several uncomfortable moments Seekamp watched him. Then the principal nodded as if Alex's silence confirmed whatever he had suspected. He leaned back in his chair. "That's all, Alex."

For the rest of the day Alex was in Panic City. Almost immediately after leaving Seekamp's office he started letting the kids at school know he was taking an "extended vacation" from dealing. During lunch he cleaned out his locker, searching for loose joints, old roaches and roach clips. What he found was deposited in the school plumbing system for permanent safekeeping.

After school Alex removed from his car and room at home every trace of marijuana as well as every device used for its consumption or processing—pipes, rolling papers, baggies, a strainer, and a postage scale were thrown out. He was so full of anxiety and nervous energy that he could hardly wait until dark to go into the backyard, dig up the jar of angel dust and grass, and rebury it in the remotest part of the property. He dug the hole extra deep and covered it with leaves.

During the week he looked for Michael behind the utility garage, at the McDonald's in town, and around the train station. He also called Michael's house three times, but each time Michael's mother stayed on the phone only long enough to say she didn't know where her son was before hanging up.

SIXTEEN

The following Saturday Ellen wanted to go for a drive. Although Alex had just driven for an hour to get to her house, he didn't mind getting back in the car. Just as long as he was with her and far away from Deepbrook, he didn't care what they did. The whole week after his meeting with Seekamp had been spent in nerve-racking paranoia while he waited to see if he would be busted. Had Alex not gotten away he was almost certain he would have gone nuts.

Sitting next to him, wearing a navy blue jogging suit and sneakers, Ellen told him about the play she was directing. As they drove down the beach road, passing the high dunes topped with dune grass, she explained that she really wanted to be a movie director, but they didn't make movies at her high school. Directing a play was the closest she could come.

The play was *The Zoo Story* by Edward Albee and it concerned two men who meet at the Central Park Zoo. They're both pretty miserable people, she explained, and the more miserable of the two winds up getting the other man to kill him.

94

Ellen's drama advisor had picked the play and Ellen said that while she neither understood nor liked it very much, she thought it was a good experience because it was not only her first chance to direct but her first chance to direct boys.

Alex smiled. Considering how easily she handled him in their relationship so far, he couldn't imagine her having much difficulty. He kept this thought to himself.

Then they talked about jogging and she told him she ran three or four miles a day. Alex didn't like to jog. He thought it was tedious and boring. When she asked him if he jogged, he said no and didn't expand on his feelings. Ellen dropped the subject.

They tried basketball next. Ellen said she really loved the Knicks and watched almost every game. It was the one thing she was allowed to watch on television after 8:00 P.M. She said she thought basketball players had the best body control of any of the professional athletes. On the court some of them looked more like dancers than ball players, she said.

Alex nodded in agreement. He was pretty sure he'd never watched more than ten minutes of a basketball game in his whole life.

The topic of basketball was benched.

Then for a while they drove around in that uncomfortable kind of silence only new lovers and strangers at parties can relate to. Finally, as if giving it one last try, Ellen asked him if he played on any high school teams.

Alex had not told her about his tennis or that the Deepbrook team was the state champion, because he didn't want to leave himself open for any questions that would be difficult to answer. But now, for the sake of having a conversation, he told her he had played on the championship team.

95

"The county champions?" she asked.

"No . . . the state," he said. He'd driven inland, keeping the car on thin country roads that took them past pretty saltbox houses and small farms.

Ellen thought for a moment. "You must be very good."

"Some people think so," he said, feeling more uncomfortable because Ellen was bound to ask what everyone else always asked him.

"Were you the best on the team?"

He nodded.

"And if you won the state championship, you were the best in the state?"

"Second best," he said. "I lost in the finals, but the team won on overall points." He hoped she'd drop it at that.

"Did you win this year?"

Alex winced. Now he had to tell her that he'd dropped off the team. But he didn't want to tell her what he'd told everyone else when they asked why. He didn't want to say, "For personal reasons" and leave her wondering. So instead he told her what being the second-best high school player in the state was really like. What a huge responsibility it was and how he was expected to continually beat back all kinds of challengers and how everybody watched him when he played and how he got the feeling some of them wished he would lose.

He told her about all the stupid demands made on him. To appear for photo sessions and interviews by the school and local papers, the benefit dinners he had to attend, and the days his coach "volunteered" him to teach tennis to underprivileged kids at clinics.

He talked about how since he was five years old his father and tennis teachers had pushed him to practice and compete and how he'd lived in fear of not getting ranked each year in a junior age group. And the pressure had never stopped. In fact, after they'd won the high school championship it had doubled. People didn't simply hope the Deepbrook team would successfully defend the championship this year, they *expected* it. And because the boy who had beaten Alex last year had graduated, they expected Alex to be the new state champion.

Then he told her why he quit, how he'd begun to question why he complied with all the bullshit. Was it for himself or for his parents and coach and Deepbrook High that he'd worked so hard? And he found he couldn't answer that question because he'd always played tennis without questioning why, without asking himself who he was playing for.

After seven years of everyone demanding that he eat, drink, and sleep tennis, he'd finally gotten sick of it. Still, he signed up for the team again in his senior year because he was expected to. But halfway through his first match, against an opponent he was clearly beating, Alex had suddenly lost the desire to win and, to his team's horror, had played the rest of the match so listlessly that his opponent won four straight games to win the first set and took the second set at love. The following day Alex resigned.

"I promised myself that day that I wouldn't play again until *I felt* like playing tennis again," he said. But inside he was worried that Ellen, like everyone else, would think he was a quitter.

Instead Ellen did a most surprising thing, she leaned over and kissed him.

"What was that for?" he asked.

"I think you know," she said, putting her hand over his.

But Alex wasn't sure. "How about a hint?"

"Because you stood up against everybody and did what you felt was right," she said.

Alex turned and smiled at her. She was the first person to look at it that way. He wasn't even sure he had looked at it that way before. He squeezed her hand and kept driving, feeling so happy that he was embarrassed to let her know.

That night after dinner, they retired to the room by the sea and Alex built a fire. They sat and talked and after a while he kissed her. This time she didn't stop him. He enjoyed kissing her. She was responsive, but not sloppy, and he could tell that she was enjoying him, too. Keeping the previous week's experience in mind, however, he didn't attempt to go further. He'd obviously made some progress since then and there was no reason to rush.

It felt like they kissed for a long time. Alex finally stopped because his lips had begun to feel sore. Ellen snuggled up against him.

"I'd like to ask you a personal question," he said.

"Okay."

"I'm surprised a girl with, uh, like you isn't seriously involved with someone."

"I could say the same about you."

"I'll tell if you'll tell," he said.

Then Ellen did something he found rather odd. Instead of telling him right away, she started kissing him again and continued very passionately for a while, making Alex wonder if she was preparing him for something she thought might upset him. His lips began to ache, but fortunately she didn't insist on kissing for too long.

"I was going with someone until Christmas," she said. "He's

a freshman at Yale. We went together all last year, but it didn't work out."

Well, that explained a few things, Alex thought, but it left some other things unexplained. "What does 'didn't work out' mean?" he asked.

"He was too demanding."

Alex knew what too demanding meant because Fran Jamison used to say that about him each time he tried to reach under her blouse.

"He wanted me to spend the weekend with him at Yale," Ellen said. "He said I could tell Poppa I was going to visit friends, but I didn't want to do it. I think he felt pressured by the other boys there. He kept telling me that his roommate's girlfriend visited almost every weekend from Albany. As if I had to do everything she did."

"How did it end?"

"He went to Europe with us over Christmas," she said. "Every day he tried to get me alone. It would have been annoying if it wasn't so funny. One day he pretended he was sick and asked me to stay at the hotel with him while Joyce and Poppa went skiing."

"Oh, God."

"I knew he was faking but I couldn't refuse. All morning he talked and talked, trying to persuade me. I think he gave himself a one o'clock deadline because as soon as the steeple bells rang he did try something and then we had a fight and I locked myself in my room. When I came out he was gone."

"He left Europe just like that?"

Ellen nodded. "It wasn't easy to explain to Poppa. A few weeks ago I got a letter from him apologizing, but I haven't answered it."

Of course Alex wanted to know why she hadn't slept with the Yalie and what *his* chances were, but he didn't ask. He knew Ellen wanted to hear his story.

The circumstances were simple, but he couldn't tell her the precise truth, which was that after he'd broken up with Fran he'd gone out with a girl named Alice Dodson, who, to put it modestly, didn't know what "too demanding" meant. The problem with Alice was that the only thing they could do together was have sex. She seemed interested in nothing except clothes, hair styles, and being seen with him. She constantly hinted about marriage and sometimes reproached him for not being affectionate in public. Alice used a diaphragm and Alex was always careful to make sure it was in place before they made love. One afternoon at her house she'd insisted it was in even though he couldn't feel it. Later she went to the bathroom and Alex checked the drawer where she hid it. Sure enough it was there in its case. He got dressed and left her crying at her front door. A week later she called and threatened to get pregnant by someone else and claim it was his baby. He had wished her luck.

Alex told Ellen the story, leaving out the sex altogether, saying Alice and he had broken up because she wanted to get engaged.

SEVENTEEN

That February Alex and Ellen worked with Gunther on the sailboat, took long walks on the beach, and visited the small, winter-slim south shore towns that would soon become heavy with summer inhabitants.

Alex was a regular Saturday dinner guest at the Schapmann's. After leaving late Saturday night only to return Sunday morning for several weekends, he had been invited by Gunther, no doubt at Ellen's urging, to stay overnight in the guest room.

But Alex quickly discovered that the invitation to spend the night did not mean that Ellen was willing to spend it with him. In fact, she had a unique knack for stretching out the steps of sexual procedure almost to the point where each weekend Alex felt he made some progress, but never seemed to get anywhere.

Other factors slowed the pace; it was practically impossible for them to be "safely" alone. Gunther had decided that it wasn't yet time to allow Ellen to visit Alex for the weekend at his house, especially since his parents were never there. Gunther also paid unexpected visits to the room by the sea late on Saturday nights when Alex and Ellen liked to sit by the fire.

The idea of messing around in the BMW was distasteful to both of them (admittedly more so to Ellen than Alex), and besides, the February and March weather that year was seasonably cold, and the icy car seats tended to dull one's sexual interests.

Toward the end of March Alex packed the trunk of the BMW with his sleeping bag and a couple of old army blankets and Ellen and he sneaked down to the beach after dark (she told Gunther they were going to the local movie theater).

Conditions were barely tolerable. Cold, damp sand quickly found its way into the bag to rub against whatever bare skin became available, and the waves seemed to reach closer and closer with each foaming crash toward shore. Still, Alex was beginning to think the beach assault might someday work. Just in the past two weeks since they'd started coming to the beach on Saturday nights, he had advanced from not being allowed to put his hand inside her blouse to being allowed unlimited access not only to the area beneath the blouse, but beneath the brassiere as well. At times Alex felt a little ridiculous, considering only six months before he had been sleeping regularly with Alice Dodson, but never did he think his time with Ellen was wasted. After all, with Alice the only thing he could do was screw, but with Ellen, sex was just part of something larger, just a slice of the whole pie. Though, frankly, Alex had to admit he was getting hungrier for that slice all the time.

"I'm not going to lose my virginity until I go to college," Ellen said matter-of-factly one night after stopping Alex's hand from its first attempt at explorations below the equator.

Alex rolled on to his back and looked up at the sky full of stars.

"It's just something I'd rather not do, knowing I'd have to face my father and sister the next morning," Ellen added.

By not saying anything Alex let her know he was peeved.

"See the bright one," Ellen said, pointing to the sky. "Straight above us and a little to the right? That's not a star, that's Jupiter."

Alex said nothing.

"Alex, don't do this."

Alex breathed deeply. "You know what kills me?" he said. "It's the way you have your whole life planned. It's like scenes from a movie you're directing. You know exactly how everything will be and you refuse to let anything happen otherwise."

"Only with certain things," she said.

Alex turned and looked at her in the dark. "Why?"

"Why not? Some things you only do once in life. I don't want to go through life with some awful memory of making love for the first time on a freezing cold beach, getting scraped by sand and maybe soaked by a wave."

Alex didn't feel up to arguing for the potential excitement of making love in their current situation. Honestly, he wasn't too thrilled with the surroundings either. Still, he was pissed off. For one thing, Ellen had said she wanted to go to college at the University of Southern California in Los Angeles, which meant that unless she sent him a plane ticket he wasn't going to get to sleep with her at all.

"Isn't there anyplace else where you can go to school and learn to become a director?" Alex asked.

Ellen hugged him. "Sometimes you sound just like Poppa," she said. "I've also applied to Carnegie-Mellon in Pittsburgh and Connecticut College, but for directing and film, USC is the best place."

Alex sighed and looked up at the star Ellen said was Jupiter. It looked like a plain ordinary star to him, but if Ellen said it was Jupiter, then it probably was.

"Where have you applied?" Ellen asked him.

"Uh, Columbia," Alex said. He wasn't sure why he didn't tell her the truth, except that maybe he hoped that if she saw he was staying in the East she might decide to also. Besides, Ellen knew exactly what she wanted to do and where she wanted to go, and it made Alex feel a little dumb that he didn't even know what he was going to do that summer, much less for the whole next year.

"What are you going to major in?" Ellen asked.

Major? What were his choices? Dope smoking 112, nine credits of sleep, intercollegiate sex. "I think I'll study psychology."

"You mean become a psychiatrist? Go to med school?"

"Uh, sure, why not?" Maybe he should have told her the truth. He didn't think she'd be disappointed, but he felt that if she had things so well planned, maybe he could, too. He decided to talk to his guidance counselor about psychiatry.

EIGHTEEN

Spring at Deepbrook High meant going out behind the utility garage during lunch period to smoke cigarettes and joints. Sometimes it got so crowded back there that it seemed more kids were out smoking than in the cafeteria eating. But that spring, no matter how crowded it got, Alex was always aware that Michael wasn't there.

More than a month had passed since Alex had last seen Michael, and although the passing of time had proven to Alex that he need not worry so much about being busted, he was still concerned with his friend's whereabouts. He had called Michael's house several times, but each time the response had been the same. Michael's mother said she didn't know where Michael was and quickly hung up before Alex could ask any more questions.

It had only taken a few weeks' absence for the rumors about Michael to start. Michael was the kind of person who inspired lots of speculation and rumor. And around high school, where appearances were always greater than reality, much of what was conjectured about Michael one day came back as the sworn truth the next.

Soon Michael was involved in everything that had or could have happened. He'd been busted by the police, he'd been killed by the Mafia for infringing on their drug trade, he'd gone mad and been put in an insane asylum, he'd run away to California, he'd joined the Moonies. The possibilities were as endless as they were silly. He was immediately made suspect of any unsolved crime. When a restaurant fire in a town nearby killed two people and the police suspected arson, Michael was the arsonist. A series of house burglaries both in Deepbrook and Upper Deepbrook were, of course, attributed to him. A gas station was robbed and a Deepbrook woman raped on the same night—around school they said Michael had gone berserk.

One Monday, after another weekend with Ellen, Alex went out behind the utility garage for a smoke. Drex Green, the human leech, was there.

"Hey, Alex," Drex said, picking a pimple on his neck, "did you hear about Michael?"

Alex looked up, not bothering to answer since he knew Drex would tell him anyway.

"Karen Donovan's mother is a volunteer at Hillcrest and she said she saw him there last week in the drug clinic," Drex said. "Where they put the heroin addicts."

Alex nodded. Hillcrest was a nearby mental institution, and for all Alex knew Michael might be there, but he doubted the part about the heroin. Not because Michael wouldn't take heroin, but because Michael and he had spent enough time together that Alex would have known.

Later in the period James appeared behind the garage. As an honors student, James was allowed to do independent study during his last semester at high school. As a result he divided his time between the library and the utility garage.

"Oh-oh. Thou has the long face of woe," James said.

"I wish I knew what happened to Michael," replied Alex.

James shrugged. "Perhaps he spontaneously self-destructed. He's been preparing for it for years."

"Look, James, he's a friend of mine," Alex said.

James nodded. "An unfortunate choice."

Alex dropped the conversation and lit a cigarette. There was something else he wanted to talk to James about. "I just found out you have to have *at least* a three point eight average in college to get into med school," he said.

"So what else is new?" James asked.

"What else?" Alex said. "Jesus, James, Ellen thinks I'm going to go to med school to be a psychiatrist. You know I've never had better than a three point in my life."

"That is because you have never applied a milligram of gray matter to academia," James said. "You are a classic case of underachiever, seemingly content to go through life with everyone except your closest friends thinking you're just another dumb blond. By the way, I called you Saturday night. Lucille said you were visiting Ellen."

"I told you last week I was going."

"Just checking, that's all," James said. "I witnessed a new low in pornography at the Triple-X theater in Deepbrook. It was called *Lesbian Hockey Brawl*. They alternately beat each other up and then impaled themselves on hockey sticks."

"Sounds gross, James."

"Meanwhile you were satisfying your libido with Ellen, no doubt."

"No doubt none of your business."

"Perhaps so," James said, leering, "but I can tell she makes your wienie hard."

"Gross, James."

"All right." James raised his hands as if in defense. "I'm only venting my jealousy. By the way, while we're on that topic here's some info to boost your overstuffed ego. I had to make a token appearance at the honor society meeting last Thursday and an old friend of yours, one Fran Jamison, asked about you."

"What did she want to know?"

"It wasn't easy to tell at first," James replied. "Her questions were vague and typically obtuse, but I began to sense what she was hinting at and told her you were involved."

"So?"

"Well, she was visibly disappointed."

"I thought I was on her shit list anyway," Alex said, "because I was contributing to the delinquency of the class."

"Alex, you've quit, remember? You haven't sold an ounce of grass in a month. Rumor has it you've reformed. If there was another class election you could run on the Born Again Straight ticket."

They paused in their conversation while James undid his sneaker to dump out a pebble.

"Where did you apply to college, James?" Alex asked.

"Harvard, Princeton, Yale, and Johns Hopkins."

"Johns Hopkins?"

"Excellent pre-med program."

"Oh, right, gynecology. I forgot."

"No, no," said James as he retied his sneaker. "I'm going to be the world's first discount brain surgeon, thereby performing the most valuable functions—preserving life, thought, and bank account."

"Seriously?" Alex asked.

James stood up. "It strikes me that the cost of good medical care in this country is too high, if you want to be serious. This is especially true of specialists' work. Why should money be the deciding factor between whether a person has a good brain operation or spends the rest of his life as a vegetable? If you screw up a leg operation you lose a leg, but if you screw up a brain operation, poof, all gone."

"I'm impressed, James," Alex said.

"Don't be," James said, "that's all verbatim from my college application bullshit. By the way, what are your plans?"

"Don't know," Alex said. "I just can't see going to college. The only good thing about it is that you get away from your parents, but mine are away all the time anyway."

It irked Alex to see so many of his classmates mindlessly following the paths set before them. To college, to marriage, to careers. Even those who appeared to deviate did so only in acceptable, society-approved ways. Instead of going to college they were taking a year off to work for a congressman or join the Norwegian navy or pick fruit in California. It was all set, all prepared, all acceptable, all mindless.

"You know," James said, "if you don't like the way things are you can try to change them. You don't have to go to college to do that."

Alex stamped out his cigarette. "I just don't know what I want, James."

"I know you don't," James said. "The problem is, my friend, that out there exists a society whose mores and values lean more heavily on the Western notion of what one does rather than the Eastern notion of who one is. Subsequently there exists continuous pressure to define oneself by one's doingness rather than one's beingness."

Alex gave James a dubious look.

"In other words," his curly-haired friend said, "unless you plan to be a Tibetan monk you'll probably have to make some kind of decision between now and graduation."

NINETEEN

On Friday Drex Green rushed up to Alex in the hallway. "Michael's back," he announced. "And he was in Hillcrest like I said."

Alex cut his next class and went out to the utility garage. There he found Michael telling a bunch of kids stories about life in the nut house. "See," he was saying, "the only difference between the patients and the doctors in that place is the doctors are the ones that carry keys." A couple of the kids laughed. Others gazed at him with astonished looks on their faces. Like Alex, they'd never known anyone who'd been in a mental hospital.

"The thing about being in the nut house, man, is there's more dope inside than outside," Michael told his entranced audience. "I was havin' so much fun I didn't want to leave."

He was in fine form, Alex thought. There wasn't a hint of that near-hysterical lunatic Alex had left at the train station more than a month before.

Later he and Michael went off alone to have a cigarette.

"I'm sorry about what happened at the train station," Alex said sincerely. "I lost my temper."

Michael shrugged but then grinned. "Yeah, well, I was pretty far off the wall then."

"I heard you were in the ward for heroin addicts," Alex said.

Michael lit a new cigarette off the butt of the one he'd been smoking. "Yeah," he said, "I was playin' around with it. I wasn't hooked or nothin'. But my old lady found my set of works and freaked out."

"I called a couple of times," Alex said, "and your mother said she didn't know where you were."

Michael laughed bitterly. "Well, what did you expect her to say? 'I just put Michael in the nut house and he won't be home for a while'?"

Michael was right, but Alex still found it hard to believe that after all that time Michael was back and nothing had happened.

"You know," Alex said, feeling relieved that Michael was all right, "I was so sure you'd been busted and I'd be next. I was going nuts trying to figure out what happened."

Michael laughed again and punched Alex playfully in the arm. But he didn't say anything more.

That night Alex went out to the backyard and after digging enough holes to plant a small forest of trees, found the jar of dope. Leaving the angel dust, he took some of the marijuana back to the house.

Before driving out to Southampton the next morning, he rolled a couple of joints. He and Ellen had been going together for almost three months and he thought they were getting to know a lot about each other, but the subject of drugs had yet to come up. Something about Ellen's manner seemed to

112

inhibit it, but Alex wasn't sure whether she was against drugs or had never tried them or was just nervous about using them around her house.

That evening he and Ellen made their usual feigned departure for the local movie theater. (Gunther disliked movies and rarely asked what they saw, but to be on the safe side, Alex always brought the *Times* review of whatever movie was playing at the Southampton movie house. They would study the review in the vanity light of his car before returning home, just in case there was an interrogation awaiting them.)

They left the car in a parking area on Sea Spray Drive and walked down to the beach, their arms full of blankets. Alex was acutely aware of the joints in his pocket, and as they laid the blankets out he entertained the thought that perhaps, if Ellen smoked a little grass, she might even be more amenable to "going all the way."

They got in between the blankets and kissed for a while. Alex kept debating when to introduce the joints and kept putting it off. He was opening the buttons of her blouse when she said, "Wait, Alex, did you hear this week?"

"Hear what?"

"Oh, come on." She nudged him playfully with her elbow.

"Give me a hint," he said.

"You know, college," she said. "Really, Alex, sometimes you seem so lackadaisical about it, I wonder if you're going at all."

"Oh, yes, college. It slipped my mind."

"Well?"

"Uh, everything's fine and dandy."

"You mean Columbia accepted you!?" she hugged him joyfully.

"Oh, sure, I never doubted it," Alex said. "How about you?"

113

"USC accepted me, Carnegie-Mellon too. I'm so happy."

"That's great," he said. "I guess you're on your way to becoming a famous movie director."

"And you'll be a famous psychiatrist." She hugged him again.

"Uh, sure." He had about as much chance of becoming a famous psychiatrist as Richard Nixon had of being reelected President. He felt for one of the joints. "Tell you what, why don't we celebrate."

"Okay."

He put the joint between his lips and lit it with El Zippo.

"What are you doing?" she asked.

"Well, I thought we'd share a joint."

"Okay."

Alex took a deep toke off the joint and handed it to Ellen, who did the same. Instead of handing it back quickly the way some nervous beginners did, she kept it until he was ready for another toke. Alex held his breath, keeping the smoke in his lungs, but something funny was going on. He didn't really want to get high. He'd wanted to see if Ellen smoked grass, but he hadn't actually wanted to get stoned with her. He always had such a good time with her anyway, it didn't seem necessary to get stoned. When she handed the joint back to him, he didn't take another toke.

"You sure you want to get stoned?" he asked.

Ellen turned and looked at him. It was a bright, cloudless night and he could see her face clearly. "Don't you?"

"Not really," he said. "Do you mind if I put it out?"

"No."

He stuck the joint into the sand. "You know that morning we met in Brooklyn," he said. "I was there to buy grass."

"When I tried to figure it out," Ellen said, "that was one of

114

the possibilities. Did you buy it from the Rastafarians?"

"Who?"

"The people who live in the house across the street from the bakery," Ellen explained. "They all wear their hair in long dreadlocks. It's part of their religion. So is smoking pot. Sometimes in the summer they sit out on the front lawn and smoke pot all day. Poppa once called the police about them. You know, I don't think Poppa believed your story about being lost. Are you a dealer?"

"I used to be a pretty big dealer," Alex said.

"What happened?"

"I don't know. Too many people found out, for one thing. Even the principal at my school. But it also lost its charge. I used to get a bigger kick out of it. I felt like I was proving something I'm not sure about anymore."

"You've stopped?"

"Pretty much, yeah. I've just got to unload some stuff that's left over. It's worth too much to throw away."

Ellen rolled over and curled against him. Alex opened her blouse and released the snap of her brassiere. He wiped his hands on the blanket to make sure there was no sand on them and then touched her breasts. Alex knew there was a limit on how far he would be allowed to go so he didn't rush. He'd been touching her breasts, fondling them, kissing them every weekend for more than a month now, and it was a kind of game to see how many different ways he could approach them—with Ellen facing him, with her back to him, with both of them lying on their backs, with her lying on top of him. Then there were variations on what he could do with them. He could press, squeeze, rub, caress them with his fingertips, scratch lightly with his fingernails and duplicate several of those actions with

115

his tongue and lips. He could settle down with one breast, or alternate between both, or even attempt to tend to both at the same time.

It was a game now, but he knew if she didn't let him progress from points A and B to point C pretty soon he was going to go stark raving loony. For the last two weekends he had toyed with her breasts for a while each night and then slowly slid his hand down her smooth stomach. But every time, just as his hand was about to slip under the waistline of her jeans, her hand would come down and, without a word or reproach from her lips, stop it.

Of course, he and she knew he'd try again tonight. Progress was the key to life. Progress was sanity; experience no progress and you went insane. In sex, in tennis, in dealing, in everything Alex did, he could never just sit back and cruise. His parents had programmed him for progress and success. He could not just play tennis for fun, he had to get better and better and beat more and more players. Just as his father had never been satisfied with Razal Dazal, Inc. and had to build it bigger and bigger; just like his mother, who had to keep running for more important offices, he had moved up in tennis and now in drugs, to larger amounts of grass and then to more potent drugs like angel dust.

So with sex also he had to push. What would happen if he suddenly gave up and spent the next three months playing with her breasts? She would think him crazy. She would also have sore boobs.

That night he slid his hand down her stomach, and her hand, like a defense missile launched to intercept the attacker, met his at the waistline of her jeans, the borderline. But unlike previous nights, when her hand had escorted his from the target area, that night she held his hand there, impeding its progress but not altering its course. This development filled Alex with new hope and excitement.

"Alex, are you really going to college?" she asked.

Oh, Jesus, what a time to ask, he thought. "How did you know?"

"Because you didn't know acceptance letters came out this week." She put her free arm around him and brought her lips up to his ear where he could feel the warmth of her breath. "Alex, promise me you won't lie anymore. I don't care whether you go to college or not, but I can't stand it when you don't tell me the truth."

He put his arms around her and hugged. "I'm sorry. I promise."

"What are you going to do, Alex?"

"I don't know, Ellen. That's what everybody keeps asking me." His whole life there'd always been someone to tell him what to do. What tournaments to play, what courses to take, where to go on vacation. All right, so now he'd rejected all those people and their advice. He wanted the opportunity to think on his own and now he had it. "I only know the three things I don't want to be," he said, "a doctor, a lawyer and a businessman."

"Well, that's a start," Ellen said.

They both chuckled and then he kissed her some more. A few minutes later, when his hand again slid down her stomach, it met no resistance.

TWENTY

On Monday Alex met James behind the utility garage.

"Voilà!" James held up a joint wrapped in red, white, and blue paper. "A patriotic joint." He lit it, took a toke and passed it to Alex.

"No thanks." Alex lit a regular cigarette instead.

James looked surprised. "She has quite an influence on you, doesn't she?"

Alex was semi-astounded. "Sometimes I think you read minds, James."

"Simple observations of behavior and a neophyte's knowledge of life, my friend. Has she threatened to break up if you keep smoking grass?"

"No, nothing like that," Alex said. "It's just that with her I've begun to see the possibilities of living unstoned, you know?"

"And doing what instead?" James asked.

"Well, being in love. You can get high on love."

James clutched his heart and stumbled around as if he'd been shot. "My God, Alex, you should be banished to Woodstock

118

and forced to wear flowers in your hair. You sound like a hippie, a relic of the sixties, a veritable social anachronism."

"Okay, then try this," Alex said. "You can get high on sex."

"Oh, God," James moaned.

"What's wrong now?"

"If that's true I'll probably be stone cold sober for the rest of my life." James took a deep toke off the joint to accent his point.

"No way, James. You'll be a doctor and get married and have three kids and live in Great Neck."

"Are you kidding? With all the dope I've taken my kids'll have four eyes and fish tails. But tell me, you're high on sex theory . . . is there actual recent experience to back it up?"

"It's still hypothesis, James."

James held the joint up to Alex's nose. "But still no smoky dopy, huh?"

Alex shook his head. "Just don't feel like it."

James took a few more puffs and put the joint out. Alex was aware that he was spoiling James's fun by not getting high with him, but he couldn't force himself to smoke if he didn't really want to. They stood around feeling awkward for a few minutes, neither knowing what to say to the other. Finally, James pointed to the school's four tennis courts and said, "Ah, look what spring hath wrought." The gym classes had just made their annual switch from indoors to outdoors and the girls were out playing.

"Shall we?" asked Alex, starting to walk toward the courts. The momentary awkwardness now disappeared; they might disagree over the grass, but watching girls was one activity they would always have in common.

They sat down near the courts. James's Florida beauty was on the second court over and they watched her quietly. She

119

was a good player, her strokes were smooth and fluid and she moved around the court quickly.

"She could be on the girls' team next year," Alex observed.

"She plans to," James said.

Alex looked at James. "Is this conjecture?"

"Nope, straight from the lady's mouth, my friend," James said. "While you have been frolicking out in Southampton I have been nurturing a deep and meaningful intellectual correspondence with Cindy."

"What happened to the gene pools?" Alex asked.

"Fie on you, lout," James said haughtily. "There has been no consideration of mixing in such a coarse manner. Ours is strictly a platonic relationship spawned one day in the library when her pen ran out of ink and she came to me for assistance. Since then we have shared several engaging and delightful moments of conversation within the library environs."

"In other words, you haven't gotten up the nerve to ask her out on a date," Alex said.

James sighed. "Precisely."

They continued to watch Cindy until her opponent suddenly put down her racket, said a few words to Cindy and departed in the direction of the gym. Cindy was left standing alone at the net, watching the girls on the other courts play.

"Shall I introduce you?" James asked.

"Okay." They got up and walked down to the fence. Cindy met them there and James introduced her to Alex.

"What happened to your partner?" James asked.

"She said she was getting cramps," Cindy said with a Southern drawl. "I gather that's the Northern way of sayin' she's got her period and don't feel like playin'."

"Maybe Alex would hit with you," James said.

"Oh, gee, I don't know, I've heard you're pretty good," Cindy said, smiling at Alex.

"James, why don't you hit with Cindy?" Alex said. But James gave him a short hard look. Apparently the gnome was not yet to the point where he could stand on the same court with the angelic Cindy.

"He'd love to hit with you, wouldn't you, Alex?" James said, giving him a decisive jab in the back.

"Sure," Alex said. Just those last few weeks, as the weather began to turn warm, he'd been feeling more and more like playing again. Stepping on to the court he picked up one of the gym rackets. It was old and cracked and strung loosely with nylon, but he didn't care, he was just going to hit with it. This was the first time he'd been on a court since the summer before. He couldn't remember going so long without playing. And it showed. Partly because of the old racket and partly because he was rusty, Alex hit the first five or six balls into the net or way out past the baseline. But after a while he found his groove and he and Cindy had a steady rally.

They hit for about ten minutes and when Alex turned around again, several kids had joined James at the fence to watch. He turned back to Cindy and hit another ball, keeping it in play, putting it where he wanted, knowing the kids were watching. Everybody needed something they could do well. As he and Cindy hit, Alex realized it wasn't tennis he'd gotten sick of, it was the organized competition, the pressure, the way people treated him as a tennis player, that had turned him against the sport. He didn't need that crap, but maybe, he thought, he could have tennis without it.

TWENTY-ONE

That night while Alex sat at the kitchen table waiting for Ellen to call, Lucille lectured him about girls.

"One monkey don't make no show," she said, loading the dinner dishes into the dishwasher. "You're too young to put all your chips in one pile, Alexander."

If he saw the same girl more than three times in a row he got a lecture about getting too serious at his age. If he went out with three different girls in the same week he was sure to hear that he was playing around too much. And it used to be that if he didn't go out on a Friday night she would lay her hand across his forehead and feel for fever.

"It ain't natural for a boy your age to be thinkin' about only one girl," Lucille said. "Especially a boy who's got the pick of the crop."

"Ellen is the pick of the crop."

"What kind of jive is that, child? You're hardly out of diapers."

"Jesus, Lucille, I'll be eighteen in two months." He stuck a cigarette between his lips and lit it with El Zippo.

Lucille frowned. "How many times do I have to tell you I don't like smokin' in the kitchen, Alexander."

"I'll only smoke half."

The phone rang. Lucille answered. "Alex, yes, he's right here." She covered the receiver with her palm. "It's Mr. Michael No Good Martin," she whispered disapprovingly. "You stay away from him, hear?"

Alex rolled his eyes. "The next thing I know you'll want to chaperon my dates."

"Don't bet on it, Mr. Smart Alex," Lucille said, handing the receiver to him. "If I want to watch a wrestling match I can just turn on the television."

Alex took the phone. "Hello?"

"Alex?" There were street noises in the background. Michael was at a pay phone. "Listen, you still have that angel dust?"

Alex glanced at Lucille, who was watching him closely. "So you think it's the battery, huh?" Alex said. "I've got some jumper cables. Where are you stuck?"

"I'll be at the McDonald's." Michael hung up.

"Okay," Alex said. "I'll be down in a few minutes."

"Where you goin'?" Lucille asked.

"His battery's dead. I'm going to give him a jump."

Lucille's eyes tightened on him. "That's what they have gas stations for, Alexander," she said.

"That's what they have friends for, too," Alex replied, leaving the kitchen.

Quickly and quietly he went out to the backyard and dug up the jar. If he got only his original investment of four hundred dollars back or even lost some money, Alex knew he'd be glad to get rid of the angel dust. He got into his car; ignition, radio, reverse. He backed out of the garage and drove down the driveway to Meadow Lark Lane.

Downtown Deepbrook. The golden arches came into view and Alex parked in the lot. The fast-foods palace was crowded with candidates for indigestion and it took a few moments for Alex to find Michael, who was sitting at a table in the back with a guy with a neatly trimmed beard and a light brown afro. Alex hesitated. He'd never seen the guy before; looked too old to be a high school student.

"Hey, Alex, over here." Michael waved at him. Damn it, Alex thought. Well, he'd go over and talk, but he wasn't so eager to part with the angel dust anymore, at least not when a stranger was around.

"This is Paul," Michael said.

The stranger stood up and extended his hand upwardly for the hip handshake. "Pleased to meet you, man." Alex shook his hand and sat down in a plastic chair.

"Paul's an orderly at the nut house," Michael explained. His speech was slow and syrupy and his eyelids drooped. "He and I used to get high together."

Alex watched as Michael picked up a styrofoam cup of coffee. The black liquid rippled as Michael's hand shook with slight tremors. In just the few days since Michael'd been back, Alex could already see him start to get crazy again. Tonight he was stoned out. Only the Great Nothing knew what he was stoned on.

Michael leaned across the table. "I'm gettin' up money to go to California," he whispered. "Paul wants a lot of stuff. I get it

124

for him and he pays me a commission, you know?"

Then they talked about life in the nut house some more and what Michael wanted to do in California. During the conversation Alex waited for Paul to say more, to identify himself in some way. He and Michael were running out of things to talk about and the conversation would soon turn to the dust. But Alex wasn't ready for that yet.

"So what do you do at the hospital, Paul?" he asked.

Paul smiled. "Orderly shit, man. You know, bed pans, shaves, change the sheets, mop the puke off the floors."

"How'd you meet Michael?"

"The first day he came on my ward," Paul said. "Some of these dudes, you know they're fucked up, right? But Michael here, I could see he was just on vacation, man. You should see this dude play Pong, man. Old Michael here's the ward champ."

Michael nodded vaguely and Paul tapped him on the arm. "Hey, man," Paul said, "I never knew you to be modest before."

Michael grinned. "Yeah, but this dude," he said, pointing to Alex, "is a real tennis champ."

Paul looked back at Alex. "No shit, man. You know, I play a lot myself. I ain't no champ, but I'm pretty steady. Maybe sometime you just want to go out and hit some, huh?"

"Sure." Alex was amused. Paul hadn't said anything that would lead Alex to suspect he was a narc and Michael had said he'd known him in the hospital. The three of them sat quietly for a few moments, and then Michael suggested they go out to the parking lot. They stopped by a sleek white Corvette, which apparently belonged to Paul.

"How does a hospital orderly afford one of these?" Alex asked, not caring if he was being rude. He had to know before he parted with the angel dust.

Paul was ready with an answer. "You sell a little dope on the side."

"What he means, Alex, is he keeps the whole fuckin' hospital stoned," said Michael.

Alex looked at the car again.

"I perceive your friend has a suspicious nature, Michael," Paul said. "Maybe we better forget it."

"Cool it, Paul," Michael said. "Alex and I have been workin' together for a long time. We trust each other, right?"

"Yeah." Alex shrugged. "Let's go over to my car."

Michael and Alex got in front while Paul sat behind them. "How does a high school student afford one of these?" Paul asked, as he handed four one-hundred-dollar bills to Alex.

"He sells a little dope," Alex said, giving Michael the tinfoil package of angel dust.

TWENTY-TWO

Two nights later his phone rang at 10:30. Alex figured it was James. "Hello?"

"Alex?" It was Ellen.

"What happened to the phone curfew?" Alex asked.

"He doesn't know I'm calling." She sounded upset. "Alex, he says I can't go to USC."

"Why?" This was great news for Alex, but he couldn't tell her that.

"Oh, he's made up all kinds of reasons, but the truth is he doesn't want me to go that far away."

That's two of us, Alex thought.

"It's not fair," Ellen complained. "I should be allowed to go wherever I think I can get the best training."

"But you said there are good schools in the East," Alex said.

"Yes, Alex, but you know how it works. Everything in film happens on the West Coast. That's where you have to be. I could go to school here, but I'd still have to go out there someday, and when I did all the kids who went out there to college and have already made the contacts would be way ahead of me. Oh, I'm so mad at him, Alex, what should I do?"

She was *asking* him what to do. Talk about switches.

"What have you done in the past?" he asked.

"I don't know, we've never really had anything like this before," she said. "He has this idea that once I go out there I may come back to visit, but I'll never really come back."

There was a pause in their conversation. Alex wondered how he could convince her to stay on the East Coast but at the same time try and support her argument against her father. It pleased him that she'd called to ask his advice, but he wondered if she envisioned him as an expert in the field of disagreeing with parents. He certainly had enough experience, but somehow that wasn't exactly something he thought he should be admired for.

"I hate him so much," Ellen said angrily.

Alex could not believe what he'd heard. "Is this Ellen Schapmann I'm speaking to?" he asked in jest.

"Oh, okay, I love him but tonight I hate him."

"That sounds more like her," Alex said. "What do you think you'll do?"

"I don't know, Alex. I'll have to try to talk to him again."

She was still intent on going West. Alex was disappointed. Didn't she realize how much he cared for her? And he knew she cared for him. Why would she want to go so far away, he wondered. Could a career in directing be that important? Could any career be that important to anyone? Alex wondered if there was something wrong with him because he lacked the ambitions Ellen and James had.

Then Ellen whispered something he couldn't hear.

"What?"

"I said Poppa and Joyce are going away next weekend," she whispered. "For a whole day."

"For a whole day?"

"They'll be back late Saturday night. He's taking her to see a riding camp in Vermont she may go to this summer."

"What do you want to do?" he asked.

"Something I told you I didn't want to do before."

Alex was momentarily stunned. "Why?"

"I changed my mind."

"I hope you're not fooling around," he said. "If you say yes now and no later it's about the creepiest thing you can do." He felt a bit angry that she'd just go and decide like that without even discussing it with him. It made him feel as if he'd had nothing to do with the decision.

"Why are you mad?" she asked.

"I don't know," Alex said. "I guess I just don't understand. I mean, first you told me you wouldn't do anything until you got to college and now you've suddenly changed your mind and I happen to be around so I'm the one who gets the honor."

"No, Alex, it couldn't be anyone else," she said. "I would have waited until college, but I want you to be the one."

"Jesus, I guess I better come prepared, huh?" he whispered. Not that anyone was listening.

"Oh, Alex."

Dreamy visions of her soft warm skin tickled his imagination. "You know, I really like you a lot," he said.

"I like you, too."

"See you Saturday morning."

"Yes."

A silence as sweet and thick as honey kept them stuck to the phone.

"Sometimes I think about you too much," he confessed.

She giggled.

"No, really. I mean it's not good for anyone to think about anyone else too much."

"Well . . . then don't." She affected a little hurt.

"But I like to." He was just about ready to make out with the telephone.

"I better go before Poppa decides to use the phone."

"Okay, bye." Alex sat back in his chair. There would be no more nights on the beach wondering how far he'd get. No more waistline interceptions. He was going to go all the way. And for the first time it would be with a girl he really liked.

TWENTY-THREE

Early the next morning Alex woke instantly. Downstairs the doorbell rang again. The digital clock beside his bed glowed 6:45. He got out of bed unable to imagine who could be at the door. A neighbor in distress? He slipped on a pair of jeans and went downstairs.

He turned the latch and pulled the front door open. A large red-faced man with a blond crew cut, wearing an olive raincoat, stood outside in the gray light. In one hand he held a wallet with a gold badge.

"Alexander Lazar?" the man asked, peering past him into the depths of the large dark house.

"Yes?"

"This is a warrant for your arrest." He held up a white legal-sized piece of paper.

There were footsteps on the stairs. "Who is it at this hour, Alexander?" he heard Lucille ask. The footsteps stopped and the detective and the housekeeper stared at each other.

"Who are you?" Lucille asked, tightening the belt of her robe.

"Lieutenant Albert Dougherty, Bureau of Criminal Investigation, ma'am," the man said. "Alex is under arrest."

"What for?"

"Selling drugs, ma'am."

Alex pretended he was reading the warrant, but he was too shocked to understand the words.

"Oh, my Lord," Lucille muttered. Alex could almost feel her eyes burning down on him. "Close the door, Alexander," she said. "You'll catch a cold standing in the draft without no shirt on."

Inside Alex waited for Dougherty to do something, but the detective stood in the hallway looking befuddled.

Lucille cleared her throat. "Well, Detective Dougherty, unless you're in a hurry, why don't you come in for a moment and have a cup of coffee. Give Alexander some time to get dressed."

Dougherty mumbled something about his partner and waved out into the dark. Alex took the cue and went back upstairs, avoiding Lucille's eyes as he passed her on the steps. In his room, he sifted through the clothes in his closet. He knew what to wear to weddings, funerals, his mother's political functions, and Palm Beach parties. But what did you wear to get busted in? What would Emily Post say?

He chose the same jacket and tie he'd worn to the theater and stopped in the bathroom to brush his teeth and comb his hair. A dozen panicked thoughts crowded into his mind. He hardly had time to consider one before the next pushed it aside. Was Paul a narc? Were they going to put him in jail? Should he run down the back stairs and try to escape? Would his parents have to be told? He even thought about the English test Miss Mormon had scheduled that day. Could he get busted and still get back to school in time to take it?

Lucille, Lieutenant Dougherty, and his partner, a small man with sly foxy eyes, were sitting in the kitchen, having coffee. The cops got up when Alex walked in.

"We have to take him in now," Dougherty said, staring at Alex's choice of clothes.

With Alex in front, the detectives and Lucille formed a small procession to the front door. Outside, the sun flashed through the trees. Lucille stayed in the doorway and watched as Dougherty and the fox led Alex away.

In the back seat of the sedan, a new question repeated itself over and over like a scratched record: Was it Michael? Had his own friend set him up? Alex couldn't believe that Michael would do that to him, but as he thought about it he couldn't figure out any other logical explanation. Alex shifted from one uncomfortable position to another and looked at the men in the car with him. He was sure the detectives knew the answer.

A few moments later on the main street they passed the house where Michael and his mother lived. Through the car window Alex squinted at the house, searching for a sign that Michael was there. No, he was rarely home anymore. More likely he was in Brooklyn hanging out at Chicken's or one of the mysterious places he wouldn't tell Alex about. Maybe because they didn't exist. From bluff to dare, that was the way Michael lived. You never quite knew what the truth was. But Alex had thought that after all the deals they'd made, the risks they'd taken, the crazy fun they'd had, that they'd grown to trust each other. No one ever really knew Michael, but Alex thought he'd come as close as you could get. Could he have been *that* wrong?

133

They drove up behind a large red-brick building in the county center. The two detectives got out and Dougherty opened the car door for Alex. Alex started to get out, but a flash blinded him momentarily and he sank back into the car. A hand grabbed his shoulder and gently pulled him out of the car. There were more flashes as newspaper photographers crowded around him. Publicity City. Alex ducked and pressed his chin down to his chest as Dougherty led him up some stairs and into the building.

As Dougherty slowly typed up the arrest report in a large room where half a dozen other detectives were at work, Alex learned the charges against him: one count of possession and one count of selling a controlled substance. A D felony, Dougherty told him. When the report was completed, he was taken to another room where he was fingerprinted and then to yet another room where he was photographed front and sides, mug shots.

Later he and Dougherty sat in a small windowless office with puke-green walls while the detective fed him a continuous flow of cigarettes and questions. Several times he asked if Alex knew where Michael was and hinted that if Alex helped them find Michael he could expect leniency in his own case.

"I don't know where he is," Alex said. In a way he felt relieved. If they were looking for Michael it meant his friend hadn't turned him in after all.

"When did you see him last?" Dougherty asked.

"I think I better talk to a lawyer," Alex answered.

Dougherty shook his head. "Listen, Alex," he said. "I don't like seeing you here. A bright kid like you with your parents got every opportunity in the world. It's tragic to blow it all. And it's worse what this does to your parents. Especially in your case.

What do you think this'll do to your mom's chances of running again? You think this is fair to her? You know what she's gonna have for a son now? A felon. Can't vote, no civil service or government jobs. Doctor, lawyer, forget it. Once you got a record, kid, you can't shake it."

Alex sighed. What did Dougherty expect him to do? Repent? Ask forgiveness? Turn in his merit badges? Or simply squeal on Michael.

"But with a little cooperation on your part it doesn't have to be so bad," the detective said. "What do you say, huh? Anything about Michael Martin come to mind?"

"No, but I'd sure appreciate another cigarette."

Dougherty's expression quickly soured, but he fished a cigarette out of his pocket and gave it to Alex anyway. Then he got up, saying he'd be back in a few minutes and left the room.

Alex was still handcuffed and the cigarette between his lips burned down, ashes falling on his slacks, smoke stinging his eyes. He thought about Ellen and wished he was sitting with her on the beach behind her house. A fog rolled in over the picture he had of the two of them on the beach. Would she hate him now that he was a criminal? He took one last drag, felt the heat of the embers on his lips and spit the butt out.

It seemed like a long time passed and then a cop came in pushing a food cart. He put a paper plate with a sandwich and a paper cup filled with brown liquid on a table and unlocked the handcuffs around Alex's wrists. Then he stood near the door and watched.

"Where's Lieutenant Dougherty?" Alex asked.

The cop shrugged. "Don't know him."

Alex lifted a dry piece of white bread from the sandwich and stared at bare slices of turkey roll inside. He decided he wasn't hungry. He was thirsty, but the iced tea tasted so bitter he could not drink it.

"Thanks anyway," Alex said, pushing the cup and plate away.

The cop smirked, locked the handcuffs again and left.

When Alex thought about it, trying to figure out what would happen, he forgot about the time. He was unsure how long he had been in the room. The sandwich and iced tea must have represented lunch. Had an hour passed since then? Had three hours passed? He realized that he no longer looked forward to Dougherty's return. He didn't want to know what would happen next.

Dougherty came back. "Come on," he said, helping Alex up. "It's time to go."

Dougherty walked slowly down the corridor, holding Alex by the elbow. "Alex, listen to me," he said. "Once you walk into that courtroom, you ain't gonna be able to decide what you want to do. Your dad's got a lawyer out there who'll make all the decisions. I can help you out now, if you help me. But once you're in that room, it's out of my hands."

They stopped before a large wooden door. Alex looked at Dougherty. "You might be right," he said, "but I can't take that chance, can I?"

The detective didn't answer. He knocked on the door.

When it opened Alex was looking into a courtroom. His father was the first person he saw, wearing a dark suit and sitting stone-faced in the first row of seats behind the railing. The thought of him rushing all morning to get there from Florida increased Alex's apprehensions. His father disliked

136

hurry. The old man's head was tilted low. His father had a large protruding forehead, and when he was angry or concentrating he lowered it the way a bull lowers his horns before charging. The expression didn't change when he saw his son enter the room. He only nodded slightly. It was a warning signal to Alex.

A short man with curly black hair and wearing a gray suit approached Alex. He walked with a bounce like a ballerina. Big smile, thick sideburns, an ugly pink bow tie, maybe the man was forty years old. A few feet from Alex he held out his hand for a shake. Alex frowned. The man smiled nervously, then must have realized that Alex was handcuffed.

"Oh, boy, sorry, Alex," he said with a wide toothy grin. "I didn't think they'd handcuff you. I'm Jack Abromowitz, your father's attorney. When the judge speaks, you don't have to say anything. I'll answer for you, okay?"

Alex nodded doubtfully.

In the courtroom he felt like he was an item being haggled over in a marketplace. The sale was quick. Abromowitz told the judge what a good kid Alex was, then a man called the district attorney told the judge what a bad kid Alex was. Then the judge fixed the price of bail, two thousand dollars, and Mr. Lazar rose and gave the court clerk cash. It took less than five minutes.

Later, at a pay phone in the hall outside the courtroom, his father called his mother to tell her the outcome of the arraignment.

"She's had a rough day," his father said, returning from the phone booth. "It's been a rude awakening, Alex. If you're involved in anything else that's going to get you in more trouble you'd better tell me."

"Nothing else, Dad."

"You realize what this does to your future? The bar association. You've ruined any chance for law."

Medicine, too, Alex thought. They expected a lot from someone who wasn't even going to college.

From the courthouse they walked to an old four-story brick office building a few blocks away and went upstairs to a door marked *J. Abromowitz, Atty.* A buxom blond receptionist, who looked like she stepped out of the centerfold of *Playboy,* asked them to wait. They sat on a yellow Naugahyde couch.

Alex lit a cigarette and gazed at the receptionist, at the way her breasts were tucked in but still bulged out of the low-cut blouse. Dressed for the Subtle Hustle, he thought. His mother had been doing that dance for years (albeit dressed more conservatively), slowly moving up, never appearing ambitious, but always doing the right things, being in the right places. His father had done the Subtle Hustle to the top of the wallpaper business, being vicious when no one could see, doing favors when he knew they'd repay. Abromowitz did the Subtle Hustle and so did this receptionist. Working for the best attorney. Likewise, Abromowitz had the best-looking women servants. Well, that's what they were. It was a symbiotic dance, the go-getters helping each other up their respective ladders. They danced to Muzak in elevators, to the AM radio in their cars while they screwed, but mostly to the sound of their own names, rising in the world, doing the Subtle Hustle.

"What about the tennis team?" Mr. Lazar asked.

"Huh?" Alex was still contemplating the Subtle Hustle.

"You quit this year," his father said. "Was it drugs?"

138

"No," he answered curtly, hoping the subject would be dropped.

"Maybe I haven't been paying enough attention to you."

Alex looked up at the ceiling and asked the Great Nothing to shut his father up. As usual the Great Nothing did not reply.

"I thought that at seventeen you wouldn't want attention," his father said. "I thought you'd want independence."

Silence would suffice, Alex thought.

Abromowitz walked in. Alex watched the receptionist eye the lawyer coldly. Oh-oh. The Subtle Hustle had slowed into the Office Grind.

"Come in," Abromowitz said to him. Alex stood and followed the lawyer. His father stayed behind.

In the office Abromowitz stepped behind a wide darkwood desk, removed his jacket and rolled up his sleeves. The little man had remarkably hairy arms. Alex could hardly see the skin underneath. The lawyer sat down in a high-backed chair and motioned Alex to do the same in a smaller version. Bookcases filled with leather-bound books lined the office walls. Shrinks and lawyers, he thought, all had the same offices, same bookcases.

Alex expected more of the palsy-walsy treatment, but Abromowitz suddenly leaned toward him, resting his hairy elbows on the desk. "Okay, Alex, who was the man?"

Alex didn't understand what Abromowitz was talking about. What man?

"Come on, Alex," the lawyer urged, "who was he?"

"What man?"

"The cop, the narc, the guy you sold to."

Alex told him about Paul, adding that he wasn't really sure

Paul was the narc. Abromowitz wanted to know why Alex wasn't sure and he told him about Michael.

"So your friend Michael has turned state's evidence," Abromowitz said.

Alex wanted to know what state's evidence meant.

"It means the cops must have picked him up a couple of months ago and told him if he didn't cooperate he'd spend his golden years behind bars," the lawyer said.

Alex shook his head. "No," he said. "Michael didn't know Paul was a cop. The detective this morning kept asking me where Michael was. They're looking for him, too."

Abromowitz leaned closer to Alex and, speaking softly, said, "Now listen, Alex, don't you think he did that just to make you think Michael wasn't involved. It takes months to get a kid to turn state's evidence and they want to get a lot of mileage out of him once he has."

Alex shook his head again. No, he couldn't believe that. He refused to believe that.

"Okay, Alex," the lawyer said. "Why don't you read the papers and see who else gets pinched. If you're the only one, maybe you're right. But if a lot of Michael's friends show up in print, think it over."

TWENTY-FOUR

His father and he drove most of the way home in silence. Alex couldn't think of anything to say. Things certainly were screwed up and there weren't many Alex thought he could unscrew. Abromowitz had told him to apply to college and get a summer job. Judges liked to see that a kid was busy and furthering his education. It could make a big difference in the kind of sentence he received. Alex had asked if jail was a possibility. Abromowitz had been vague in his reply.

Alex thought about the English test he'd missed. If he was going to college now, he'd need good grades. The invisible consequences of being busted began to press in on him in the car and he rolled down the window, as if the wind rushing in could blow his troubles away.

He knew his mother wasn't home the moment he stepped into the house. It was something he'd developed as a child, a Mother-Sensor. He felt a whole different set of vibrations when

141

she was there. She'd probably gone out to the beauty parlor to have her hair done after his father had called about the arraignment. That was what she did whenever she had to get away and think. When she'd been the county executive, the beauty parlor was the only place she could concentrate without the disturbances of her job. Thus she had approached all the family crises he could remember with a new hairdo.

Alex stood at the bottom of the stairs, not sure where to go next. Each way he turned he had to face people who were undoubtedly hurt or disappointed or both. There were no explanations or excuses for what he'd done. Now, having to face all the people he knew, Alex discovered he felt ashamed.

He went into the kitchen. Lucille was sitting at the kitchen table with her back toward him.

"They'll get over it, Lucille," he said feebly, sitting down at the table.

"Them, maybe, but what about you? You done it this time," Lucille said, looking away from him.

"I'm going to college," Alex said, recalling what Abromowitz had told him. Trying to appear at ease, Alex slouched down and put his feet up on a chair.

Lucille turned and two bloodshot eyes glared at him. There were dark trails on her cheeks where tears had run down. "Get your feet off that chair!" she ordered harshly, laying her hands on the table. "What kind of jive talk is that? What makes you think you gonna stay in college if you're only goin' so the police will be happy? Where's your sense, child? Most black folks I know never been past the fifth grade got more sense in their little fingers than you."

Alex sat up stiffly.

"You got to grow up now, Alexander," Lucille slapped the

tabletop. "How much longer you think your ma and pa's gonna come to your rescue? They'll quit someday. Ever think of that? Someday you gonna bite off more than they can chew."

Lucille stood up and stared angrily around the kitchen. Alex had never seen her so aroused. "What the hell's wrong with you anyway?" she asked angrily. "Look at this house," she said, spreading her arms out as if to take in the whole structure. "You got three cars in the garage, your parents buy you the best of everything, all you got to do is ask. Most of the world never even gets inside a house like this, much less lives in one. What the hell were you selling drugs for, Alexander? What'd you want that you couldn't have?"

Myself, Alex thought, knowing he could never explain that to Lucille. Not sure he could even explain it to himself, but sure that at one time it was true. Instead, to Lucille he said, "I'm going straight."

Lucille stared at him, squinting her eyes. "There you go, Alexander. Sure you're goin' straight. Straight to the devil himself. Ever since you was a little boy you been able to get sweet and sorry and do that trick. But one hand washes the other, child. You ain't trickin' no one except yourself now. This time we're all gonna wait and watch."

The front door slammed and Alex's Mother-Sensor started ticking. He heard the tap of heels in the hallway. The closet opened and hangers rustled. A moment later his mother entered the kitchen.

If she hadn't been a politician for so long she would have been beautiful, Alex thought. She was tall, but not big; feminine, but not soft; pretty, but not inviting. Because she had worked with men all the time she wore businesslike gray or blue suit outfits and had her hair done like Barbara Walters.

143

Alex noticed she was not as darkly tanned as his father. If only she'd let her hair down, put on a turtleneck sweater and a pair of jeans, she would have been a mother he could have related to.

His mother was not smiling as she stopped in the middle of the kitchen. "Lu, fix me a cup of coffee," she ordered.

"Yes, ma'am."

She sat down at the table and dropped a folded copy of the evening paper before Alex. "Congratulations," she said, not trying to hide her anger.

His eyes went straight to the headline:

COUNTY EXEC'S SON BUSTED

Beneath the headline was a picture of him being led up the steps to the courthouse by Dougherty. And the story:

DEEPBROOK—Alexander Lazar, 17, the son of former County Executive Carla Lazar, was among four alleged narcotics dealers arrested early this morning and charged with possession and sale of drugs.

Lazar, a student at Deepbrook High School, was said to be part of a ring which sold cocaine, marijuana and PCP, also known as angel dust, according to police. Others in the ring were arrested in Harlem and Brooklyn in what police say was a combined effort by city and Long Island detectives to cut off the increasing flow of drugs from the city to the suburbs.

Lazar was arrested in his parent's home on Meadow Lark Lane in Upper Deepbrook and arraigned before County Judge William McClosky. He was released on $2,000 bail.

Others arrested were:

Arno "Chicken" Blackstone, 33, of 184 Brighton Ave., Brooklyn.

Sheila Lambert, 24, address unknown.

A 15-year-old Harlem youth whose name was not released pending family court proceedings.

Mrs. Lazar, who resigned from the county to run for Congress last fall and lost by a narrow margin, arrived with her husband this morning from their Palm Beach vacation home. Edward P. Lazar, the boy's father, is a retired business executive.

Classmates of Lazar's at Deepbrook High today expressed surprise at the news of the arrest . . .

Alex put the paper down. Michael's name was not there.

"I want you to see Dr. Coleman," his mother said. Dr. Coleman was his former psychiatrist. In the past his mother had sent him to Dr. Coleman whenever he'd become too much of a hassle for her to handle. That was one thing about going to Dr. Coleman: whenever Alex went his mother could stop worrying about him and relax. Seeing a shrink didn't do much for Alex, but it was wonderful for his mother.

"Why do you want me to go?" Alex asked.

"There must be a reason why you were selling drugs," she replied, "and I doubt you understand it yourself."

"Why do you think I did it?"

His mother looked startled. "Why, I wouldn't begin to speculate. I'm not a professional."

"You must have some idea or you wouldn't suggest I see Dr. Coleman," Alex said.

He watched her bosom heave. "Honestly, Alex, if you must know, I think you're terribly afraid of growing up and leaving home. I think the trouble you're in is a subconscious attempt to get more attention and perhaps even make us punish you by keeping you home."

Why did mothers have bosoms while other women had breasts? he wondered. Maybe Dr. Coleman knew.

"So, you think I'm scared of the future."

"Really, Alex, I think you and Dr. Coleman should discuss it."

"Why can't I discuss it with you, Mom? How come every time there's a problem I get sent to someone else?"

"I can't be objective, Alex." His mother stared at him. She must have been wondering, *Whatever happened to that sweet obedient child of the past?*

"I think you and Dad have always been too involved in your own careers to want to bother with me," Alex said. "I think you want to pack me off to Dr. Coleman and hope he'll fix me up as if I were a broken toaster or something. You managed to run a whole county full of people, but you don't want to bother with me."

Her eyes widened. "Alex, how can you say that?" His mother started to cry.

Oh shit, thought Alex. Even if it was true, he probably shouldn't have said it. He began to imagine the kind of day she must have had. The unexpected telephone call from Lucille, running to the airport, flying to New York, people calling, reporters bugging her. What an embarrassment he must be to her.

"I'm sorry, Mom."

"Alex, how could you say that?" His mother wiped her nose with a tissue she'd magically pulled from her dress. "We've never neglected you." She sniffed. "We gave you everything. Why on earth did you do this to me?"

"Mom, I'm sorry. I didn't mean to do anything to you."

"Oh, you must have, you must have known what the consequences would be if you got caught."

"Mom, I swear to you, it never occurred to me that I'd get caught or that anything like this would happen."

His mother looked at him skeptically, redabbing the places

146

on her face where old tears had fallen because no new ones were appearing.

"I'm not kidding, Mom. I never sat down and said to myself, 'I'm breaking the law and this is what may happen if I get caught.' I just didn't think I was doing anything that bad."

For a few moments they both sat at the table with nothing to say. Mrs. Lazar tucked the tissue neatly back into her dress and touched her hair in several places to see if the new hairdo was staying up. Then she nodded. "Will you see Dr. Coleman?"

"I'll think about it, Mom," Alex said, but he knew the real answer was absolutely, unequivocally, no way in hell.

TWENTY-FIVE

The BMW sputtered and stalled. Alex shivered, burped up the taste of Lucille's blueberry pancakes and turned the ignition key again. The car started and he was off to school, off to face everyone.

Other cars were pulling into the student parking lot and kids were getting out and looking at him with long, piercing gazes. There was no doubting the speed at which the news of his arrest had traveled. Even the SST couldn't beat a juicy piece of gossip from one end of Deepbrook to the other. Alex picked up his books and walked alone into school. As soon as he was inside Drex Green was beside him.

"Wow, man, I heard about what happened to you yesterday." Drex reached under his shirt to pick a pimple on his back. Alex stopped at his locker to drop off his jacket and some books He ignored Drex, but as usual the kid didn't notice.

"Was it cool getting busted, huh?" Drex asked.

Alex not only heard the words, he felt them, as if a barbell had fallen on his shoulders. "Drex," he said, "I can't talk about it." He shut the locker and walked away.

His first class was study hall. Some mornings he skipped it, but this morning he needed to catch up on Shakespeare. He wanted to make up the test he'd missed the day before. After all, grades mattered now that he was going to go to college.

Alex felt two dozen pairs of eyes stare at him as he entered the room. It reminded him of a commuter train, the way all the kids in study hall were reading the paper. He sat down at a desk near the front of the room and tried to study, but the ensuing whispers ruined his concentration. Nobody talked to him, however. It seemed that those who weren't his friends were too shy to say anything and those who were friends didn't know what to say.

Although studying was fruitless, he was still determined to make up the test. Even a D would be better than no grade at all. The hall bell rang and classes changed.

Miss Mormon glared at him as if he were some kind of child molester or something. For a brief moment Alex wasn't sure how he would survive the class that day, but it turned out to be easier than he thought. Miss Mormon ignored him for the entire period.

After class Alex waited while other students asked their questions and left. Miss Mormon knew he was standing there, but when the other students had gone she sat down at her desk, still ignoring him, and began reading papers. Alex mustered his courage.

"Miss Mormon?"

The teacher put down her papers and stared at him with an expression that reminded Alex of an incensed water buffalo.

"Yes?"

"I missed the test yesterday."

"I am aware of that." Miss Mormon picked up her papers and started reading again.

"I'd like to make it up," Alex said.

"You failed, Mr. Lazar."

A great start for college, he thought. "I studied for it, Miss Mormon," he said, trying not to sound like he was pleading. "I won't fail if you let me take it."

She shuffled her papers and didn't answer.

"I was in jail yesterday," he said. "That's a legal excuse, isn't it?"

The papers fell to the desk and Miss Mormon's small, hard eyes flashed laser beams of hate at him. "You have no excuse, Mr. Lazar."

"Miss Mormon," Alex said, "regardless of your personal feelings, professionally I think you have a responsibility to give me that test."

"Please leave the room, Mr. Lazar." She stared at the papers on the desk.

"This country is based on democratic principles," Alex said. "All men are created equal regardless of race, color, creed, or arrest record."

"Get out, Mr. Lazar." Miss Mormon was turning red.

"Just imagine what might have happened had Shakespeare's English teacher not let him make up tests."

"GET OUT, MR. LAZAR!" she screamed.

Alex slammed the door behind him.

At lunchtime Alex checked for James out behind the utility garage—nothing except a couple of sophomores copping a joint. Just as he was about to return to the school building, Alex

150

thought he heard a rattle among the garbage cans lined up along the back end of the garage. He looked closer and saw two worn-out purple basketball sneakers sticking out between the cans.

James was wedged between two garbage cans, the fur-lined hood of the green aviator coat pulled low over his forehead. A wine bottle, almost empty, lay nearby.

"Hello, oppressed one," James spoke in muddy words.

"Do you drink alone often?" Alex asked.

"Only when no one else is around."

Alex picked up the bottle. Bourgogne Aligote, 1932. "Where'd you get this?"

"My parents' wine cellar. The most recent year I could find. What year is it? I mean, what period?"

"Fifth."

James peeked out from under the hood and squinted. "Gracious me, I haven't even been in school yet."

"Why are you drinking?" Alex crouched down next to James and lit a cigarette.

"To drown your sorrows," James said, smiling his sheepish little-boy smile. "I decided you'd be too distraught to get drunk, so I'd do it for you." He tilted his head toward the bottle. "Have some, and remember, if you need a character witness in court, I'll stand by you all the way."

"Thanks, but one look at you and they'd give me life."

"Alex, my friend," James said, wiping his nose on the sleeve of the coat. "You will become a better man for this. Being arrested builds fortitude. It gives you pride and self-respect."

"Sure, James." Alex took a deep drag off the cigarette and exhaled through his nose. "That goddamn Mormon failed me on a test because I was in jail."

"Maybe you need a note from the jailer."

"She'd fail me anyway," Alex said. "Listen, James, can you be serious for a second?"

"It's possible."

Alex sighed. "You can't tell anyone. You've got to swear."

"I swear." James held up his left hand.

"The lawyer told me Michael made a deal with the cops. He got me busted."

"And you don't know whether to believe him?"

"I just don't know," Alex said. Then he told James how Abromowitz had said everyone Michael knew would get busted except Michael if he'd turned state's evidence, and how it appeared to be true.

"But your lawyer doesn't know for sure," James said, "and the cops won't tell you."

"That's about it," Alex said.

James shrugged. "Can't help you, my friend."

The two-minute warning for the next period droned out of a speaker outside the school and Alex got up and gave James a tug. His friend wobbled a bit.

"So what are your short-term plans?" James asked, dropping the butt of his cigarette into the wine bottle.

"Guess I'm going to college next year," Alex said. "And I have to find a summer job."

James shuddered. "Sounds awful."

Alex nodded. "No one said rehabilitation was easy."

"What college?" James asked.

"I don't know yet. Chelonia, maybe."

"Fantastic," James said. "My brother Eddie will be your spiritual mentor. He called last night and said the whole school's been meditating for three weeks. It's very serene up there. What do you think you'll study?"

Alex shook his head. "What does it matter?"

"Well, if you knew what you wanted to do after college, you could take courses that would prepare you."

After college? Alex thought. Jesus, it had only been a day since he started thinking as far as college. Maybe there wasn't even life after college.

"I wouldn't go to college if I didn't know why I was going," James said.

"But that's why I'm going," Alex said. "Because it's college."

"College is preparation for life, Alex. You can't stay there forever."

They started to walk back toward the school building. "You know," Alex said, "I went to nursery school to prepare for kindergarten, which prepared me for elementary school, which prepared me for junior high, which prepared me for high school, which is supposedly preparing me for college, which you say will prepare me for life. How do you know you won't spend your whole life preparing for the next step. Maybe we never get there. Maybe it's all absurd."

James smiled. "Really, Alex, you're thinking too hard. Don't get so serious. Don't you know absurdity is strictly a middle-class concept?"

TWENTY-SIX

That night his parents stayed at home. Alex could not recall the last time all three of them had been in the house together for an entire evening. Not that it made any difference, though. His mother spent most of the evening reading a novel in the living room while in the den his father watched a basketball game. Alex spent most of his evening in his room trying to catch up on the schoolwork he'd neglected that semester. He had a lot to do and he tried to concentrate on it, but his thoughts kept drifting to Michael and the bust and his parents.

What were they doing, he wondered, standing guard? He couldn't imagine what they thought they were accomplishing, sitting around the house all day waiting for him to come home from school and then hanging around all night while he worked in his room. It was too late to do anything about what had already happened, and Alex could take care of what still had to happen himself. Their presence in the house made Alex aware of how self-sufficient he had become. He needed his parents for money, but little else. Applying to colleges, getting a summer job—he could do all this himself. In a way this thought made him sad. Part of him wished that something more than dollars would pass between them.

Later that night the phone rang and after several minutes Alex's father knocked on his door. "It's Abromowitz," Mr. Lazar said. "He wants to speak to you."

Alex picked up the phone.

"Alex, I've got some information about your friend," the lawyer said. "You want to hear it?"

In a way, Alex didn't want to know what the lawyer had to say. But he said he'd listen.

"Okay," the lawyer said, "now I'm reading from a confidential police report I'm not supposed to have and you're not supposed to hear about, so if anyone ever asks you, I never read this."

"Sure." Alex was not impressed by the cloak and dagger routine.

"Okay, now I'm only going to read parts of it because it's long and complicated and pretty boring," the lawyer said. "Here goes: 'In an interview after the arrest, he—that's Michael they're talking about—he confessed to several house burglaries in the Deepbrook area. These later checked out. Additional questioning revealed that the subject had carried a small-caliber weapon during the burglaries. An investigation indicated that the weapon was useless and could not be fired.' So your friend carried a gun that didn't work," Abromowitz said.

"I know," Alex said impatiently.

"You do, huh." Abromowitz didn't sound happy to hear that. "Okay, listen: 'Psychological tests indicate the subject is severely multihabituated and potentially recidivistic. The doctors who . . .' "

155

"Wait," Alex said. "What does all that mean?"

"Okay, multihabituated means addicted to a lot of drugs at once, so severely multihabituated means . . ."

"Come on," Alex said angrily. "I know what happens when you put severely in front of a word. I don't need that explained."

"Okay, just cool down," Abromowitz grumbled.

"What does recid—whatever you said mean?" Alex asked.

"Recidivistic," Abromowitz said. "It means he's a criminal repeater who probably can't be rehabilitated. That means he's probably going to spend most of his life in jail if he doesn't get killed along the way."

"I can't believe it," Alex said weakly.

"Yeah, well it's a sad commentary on the way you kids view life," Abromowitz said, his words full of scorn. "Like a game without rules. You know what Jungle Habitat is? Where they took a little bit of Africa and put it in New Jersey. So you kids took a little bit of the South Bronx and put it in Deepbrook. I can see why Michael might have been involved in this crap. The kid's a lifetime loser. But not you."

Alex didn't say anything. He didn't know what to say.

"Okay, now there's something else," the lawyer said. "You were right, the police are looking for Michael. One of the problems with turning state's evidence is that it means the cops usually have to let the guy go back into his environment to nail his buddies. Michael went in, got everyone busted and then disappeared."

"So he's gone," Alex said, almost wishfully.

"I doubt it," Abromowitz said. "He's probably back on drugs and that means he'll be stealing. We'll see him again pretty soon."

Again Alex had no reply.

"Okay, Alex," the lawyer said. "Think about it for a few days and call me back if you change your mind. The more you cooperate the easier it will be on you."

"Sure," Alex said. "Hey, and thanks for calling. I didn't mean to get mad before."

"Okay, Alex. Put me back on with your father before you hang up."

After Alex got off the phone he sat and stared out the window into the dark for a long time. Maybe he could understand Michael's turning in all the others. They weren't really his friends, and, after all, no one wanted to spend the rest of his life in prison. But he was Michael's friend. It was stupid to compile a list of things he had done for Michael, but he could have. And when it was all added up it seemed incredibly unfair that all he'd gotten in return was an arrest warrant.

TWENTY-SEVEN

His parents lasted two days more. Then at dinner one night his father announced they were going back to Florida. "We're useless up here," he said. "You're a grown boy now. We can't follow you around making sure you're good. I've talked it over with Abromowitz and he agrees. There's no point in our being up here. He'll take care of anything that comes up."

"But you must agree with some provisions," his mother said. "Let's agree that until the trial you'll come directly home from school every day and stay in all evening. No more trips to the city."

Alex looked at Lucille. He knew where his parents were getting their information.

"What about weekends?" he asked. "I've been going to Southampton."

His father swallowed and frowned. "You're not going anywhere I don't say you're going," he said, lowering his forehead. "Understand?" His father had the ability to radiate paralyzing intensity when he spoke. A great cerebral zap that produced mental lockjaw in the listener. Alex felt the inclination to fight

158

evaporate from him. "You can't afford the slightest error now," his father said. "Your future is on the line."

"Ellen's in Southampton," Alex said.

"Ellen?"

"The girl I've been going to see every weekend for the last three months."

"Oh, yes, the one whose father owns that bakery." His father thought for a moment. "All right, Alex, I don't want to make it any harder on you." He dabbed his lips with a paper napkin. "One more thing, Alex. I know this college business has been pushed on you rather hastily. But in the long run you will learn that college is one of the best things in life."

"Have you decided where you want to apply?" his mother asked.

Before Alex could answer, his father answered for him. "I think he should go to Columbia, Carla."

His mother's long red fingernails rapped the kitchen table rhythmically as she gave her husband a sharp look that Alex interpreted as saying, *Oh, yeah? What's he going to do about grades?*

"I still have plenty of friends on the board," his father said, as if he too had had the same thought. "That reminds me, I ought to make a few calls." He got up. "Alex," he said, looking through his wallet, "if you have any questions or problems while we're gone you can call Abromowitz." He handed Alex the lawyer's business card. "And, of course, you'll call us if you need anything. One of us will be coming back up in two weeks to see how you're doing." His father went upstairs to make his phone calls. He would never even try to understand why his son had been busted or consider the idea that it might be partially his fault, if any fault could be found.

159

It was the same story, Alex thought, the story of his life. He'd always been put in someone else's hands, first Lucille's, then his tennis teacher's, then Dr. Coleman's and now Abromowitz's. This was what his father had worked for, to have enough money to pay other people to bring up his son. And if they'd failed to do a good job, well, it was just another indication of how poor services in this country had become.

Alex was beginning to see what it was about his parents that he'd instinctively rebelled against. The companies, the business, the money, the politics, all the activities his parents had been involved in when they should have been involved with their son. Alex had wanted parents, but instead he'd gotten a series of substitutes.

Some things were beginning to make sense to Alex now. His quitting the tennis team, his not wanting to go to college, even the dealing. They all went against his parents because, Alex realized, he was trying his damnedest not to be grown up and like them.

Now it was his mother's turn. "Alex, will you apply to other colleges besides Columbia?" This was her nicest way of saying, *You don't stand a chance there so you better have some safety schools.*

Alex told her he'd spoken to his guidance counselor, who was checking schools that might still be accepting students.

His mother nodded. "You know, I thought about what you said."

Alex felt a tremor of nervousness.

"You may be right," she said. "Perhaps we didn't spend enough time with you, but life is different today. You can't compare the way people raised children twenty-five years ago with the way they raise them today. The demands put on people are much greater today and they simply don't have as much time as they used to. Do you understand?"

"Sure, Mom."

"You were always such a good-natured child and so well behaved that we had no reason to think anything was wrong."

Alex grinned. "Maybe I should have been bad more often, huh?"

His mother gasped slightly. "Oh please, Alex, I hope this will be all." What she really meant was, *You've made it hard enough for me to return to politics, please don't make it worse.*

"Don't worry, Mom."

She asked him if he would like her to get him a job as a summer intern in the county government or at a newspaper, but Alex said he wanted to find something on his own. Then they talked about what he might study at college and Alex began to realize that his role in this conversation was to be cooperative and make his mother feel better about leaving him alone again. And for a brief moment he got mad and wanted to tell her what a phony she, too, was, but then he calmed down, realizing that it was too late. His parents were the way they were and they weren't going to change. He was almost eighteen years old now and it was too late for them to start being parents. Maybe there were a lot of things they should have done, but it didn't matter now. On the other hand, there was really no reason for him to placate them any longer, so when his mother asked him again if he would go see Dr. Coleman, Alex said no.

TWENTY-EIGHT

Saturday morning after breakfast Alex put on his best jeans, a denim shirt, and his suede jacket. The BMW started on the first try and purred. Bingo, Ellen was just an hour's drive away. On the way he made one stop, at the drugstore in Deepbrook.

As he walked down the aisles of deodorant and toothpaste he felt a little nervous, but he really got the shakes when he saw who was behind the sales counter. No, he didn't know her, but she'd been a senior at Deepbrook the year before and she was really nice-looking with long blond hair in the California-Colorado-surfer-skier style.

His legs froze momentarily and he limped stiffy behind a display case. Jesus, did he feel self-conscious.

Hey, it's nothing to be embarrassed about, he told himself, just ask for some prophylactics and pay for them. Prophylactics? What is this, Alex, health class? Ask for condoms. Condoms? What are you, forty-five years old? Sheaths? Forget it. Rubbers? Ha, she'll give me a pair, he thought. Bags?

He glanced at the display case before him. Tampons? Better move to something more appropriate. You know about guys who hang around the Tampon displays. There, he felt safer by Dr. Scholl's foot powder. Maybe he should ask for them by name. What were the choices? Four-X, but they were smelly. Alice had carried her own supply of them before she switched to the diaphragm.

There were Trojans, Guardians, Ramses . . . Alex considered them logically. The Trojans had been guardians and they still got screwed by the Greeks and their wooden horse. Now Ramses, there was an aristocratic name, considering all that Egyptian pharaoh stuff.

Alex shook out his legs and marched up to the sales counter.

"Can I help you?" the girl asked with a smile.

"Yes, I'd like a box of Ramses." *Buzzzzz.* Inside six million volts of nervous energy surged through his synapses.

"Box of three or twelve?" Miss Calm-and-Collected asked. Not even a blink. She probably sold them to six-year-old kids without batting a peroxided eyelash.

"Three, I guess."

She knelt down behind the counter. Alex toyed nervously with the Chap Stick display and suddenly eighty little Chap Sticks flooded out on to the counter and fell to the floor. Alex started grabbing for them, bending down and picking them up.

"What happened?" The girl was leaning over the counter and looking down at him. Her breasts stuck out when she leaned over like that. He could almost reach out and touch them.

"Oh, nothing, they just all sort of fell out. I'll get them," he said.

"Here, let me help." Damn. She came around the counter.

Alex noticed she had the pack of Ramses in her hand. He felt his face growing red.

Their shoulders brushed and their eyes met for a second. Didn't she look a bit red also? Half of him felt like running away and the other half felt like crawling on top of her. He could just imagine someone walking in and finding them rolling around on the floor amid several dozen Chap Sticks. Very kinky.

Finally, they got them all and the girl went back behind the counter again. Alex sighed and stood up.

"Don't bother putting them back in the display," she said. "I'll do it later. This is a dollar seventy-five." She dropped the little box into a white paper bag.

He frowned. Only three for a dollar seventy-five?

"A dozen costs four fifty," she said as if she'd read his mind.

Nothing like encouragement, Alex thought. Besides, it was a better deal. "I'll take a dozen," he said, feeling less flustered.

She replaced the smaller box with a larger one. He dug the money out of his wallet and paid her. She smiled and handed him the bag.

"Thanks." Feeling pretty cocky now, he tossed the bag in the air and caught it.

"Any time," she said and winked.

He was just pushing open the door when he heard her call out behind him, "And don't use them all in one place."

He parked the BMW in the courtyard near the garage. The garage doors were open and there was an empty space where the old Porsche usually stood.

Ellen came out and ran toward him. A moment later she was in his arms, her breasts compressed against his chest, the taste of strawberries on her lips and her black hair smelling freshly

164

washed. After each week away, it always felt strange, holding her again on Saturday mornings. To Alex it brought back little-kid fantasies of journeying to a foreign land where the beautiful princess waited.

"I wish I could see you more than just on weekends," he said, holding her, not wanting to let go until he had to leave on Sunday.

"Me, too." She pressed her face into the bend of his neck and kissed him, causing shivers up and down his right side.

"Your dad's really gone for the whole day?" He inched his hand around her back under the sweater and felt her warm smooth skin.

"Uh-huh." She kissed his neck again. "Hope you came prepared."

"Yes." But he was surprised she'd mentioned it. Rather, he'd expected her to wait, to take some time to get used to him again. Even though only a week had passed, they were still new to each other. He slowly broke away from her arms and reached into the car for the white package lying on the front seat.

They walked, arm in arm, toward the house. Ellen seemed so serious, so committed to the whole thing. As if it was some kind of play she was directing rather than their romance. Well, he thought, maybe that was her way, even if it did make him feel like a fellow actor in a skit instead of her lover.

She led him inside, and through the open doorway at the end of the hall he saw the room by the sea. He could see the waves turning blue and sparkling in the sunlight. He would have liked to sit there with her for a while. Even just for a few minutes until he felt far away from Deepbrook and the bust and the rest of his life. But she held his hand tightly and pulled him up the wide staircase toward her bedroom with its sky-blue walls and white curtains catching the sun. And there she pulled him down to the bed.

"What about the cook?" he asked.

"He doesn't see what he's not supposed to see."

"What if your father asks?"

"He wouldn't. He's a cook, not an informer."

Alex kissed her.

"Alex?" She put her arms around him.

"Yes?"

"You know this is my first time. You'll be gentle, won't you?"

"Like Ivory Snow."

They kissed again, and although he felt the touch of her lips, she seemed distant to him, so concerned with what they were about to do that she wasn't really getting into the warm-ups. So much do it and not enough feel it, he thought. He wanted to stop and explain these feelings, but when he pulled her up straight to tell her she interpreted the message differently and took off her sweater. He might have said something then, but at the sight of her bare breasts he felt himself lose the will to interrupt.

Then his shirt was off and Ellen's jeans were on the floor and his hands were tracing the length of her long legs. Alex kissed the edge of her yellow bikini panties and heard her first moans more like light sighs as her fingers laced his hair and pushed his face down.

Then they were both naked and crawling between the cool sheets and hugging and shivering together. Kissing her slowly, he tried to savor the feeling of her lips against his, tried to stretch the time out to find some warmth between them to add to the heat of their bodies.

He stopped to put on the prophylactic. She was fascinated

166

and made him feel embarrassed when she insisted on watching him unroll it down his penis. They kissed and played again and then he placed himself between her legs, lined things up and pushed. He felt her wince and shift her hips, knocking him away. He lined up again, pushed, was deflected again.

"You can't pull away like that," he said, realigning himself.

"It hurts, Alex."

"It only hurts if you fight it."

Ellen made an effort to relax and on the next try Alex gained half an inch. But she stiffened and cried out. Somehow, it no longer seemed like sex. He felt like a machine performing a job, and not a very pleasant one either—inflicting pain. He pushed again.

"Alex, please stop, it hurts too much," she cried.

"Ellen," he whispered harshly in her ear, "if it's not this time, it'll be the next. If you put it off it won't be any easier next time." He sounded like a tape recording. Everything was becoming machinelike. A robot punching holes in aluminum cans couldn't have been more heartless. Still, he pushed again, this time going halfway in. Ellen suddenly clawed him in new pain. Another push and he was in.

Big deal.

Ellen writhed beneath him and through her tears begged him to pull out. He tried to slide up and down. She clung tightly, gasping at each rise, moaning with every ebb. Alex stopped. There was no pleasure, no purpose in harming her like that. He pulled out.

Her body went limp. He rolled off her, feeling as if he'd been deceived, not by Ellen, but by something larger and less tangible.

"I'm sorry, Alex. I'm so sorry, but it hurt so much," she

167

sniffed and put her arms around him, pulling him to her.

"It's okay," he said. "I'm sorry, too." At least he felt less like a machine and more like a human being. If it wasn't this time it could be next time, but next time would have to be better.

"I think I'm bleeding," she said, sitting up and looking down at the sheet. A dark red spot. They got up and Ellen pulled the sheet off before the stain spread to the mattress beneath. She went into the bathroom to fix herself. The pink tint of blood on the prophylactic . . . he wrapped it in some tissues. From his shirt he took a cigarette and lit it.

For Ellen, he felt bad. After all her planning she'd wound up with this. No coming together at the peak of lust, no cosmic implosions. Not even a nice memory of the first time. Instead he had hurt her, something he'd never wanted to do.

"Are you smoking?" Ellen asked from the bathroom. Just the sound of her voice stabilized his feelings.

"Yes."

She walked past him and opened a curtain. The light danced on her shoulders. She stood, her naked back toward him, looking at the ocean.

"So much for your wonderful memories of the first time," he said.

She returned to the bed and sat beside him, watching the cigarette smoke rise. "Don't be upset." She touched his neck and looked at him with those dark brown eyes.

"It didn't work," he said.

"It hurt, Alex."

"I know." He reached for her hand. "But all your plans about the right way to do it."

She smiled. "It's too late to worry about that. Maybe next

168

time you should put the thing on first and then we'll start. I felt ready at first, but when we stopped to put it on, I didn't feel right." She kissed him.

Her rationality was frightening.

"I felt that, too," he said. "But I really wanted it to be, uh . . ." What exactly had he wanted it to be? Different? Better? The ultimate? Total orgasmic disintegration? Would you believe a small nuclear reaction? Where was the Great Nothing now?

"Don't be disappointed," she whispered, stroking his shoulders. "We'll try again, later."

He should have agreed then and forgotten about it, but instead he got up and carried the bundle of tissue paper and prophylactic into the bathroom where he dropped it in the toilet. There was a face in the mirror; matted strands of hair falling over his forehead, a cigarette hanging rebelliously from the corner of his mouth, the slight reddish dot of yesterday's pimple, other traces of acnes past here and there, gray blank eyes, the protruding forehead, courtesy of his father. He scowled. This was supposed to be an adult? He tried wrinkling his forehead and spoke in a deep voice. "Son, when I was your age I had a wife, three kids, two cars, a fifty thousand dollar life insurance policy, and a perforated ulcer."

"Alex, did you say something?" Ellen asked from the bedroom.

"No, I was just practicing being an adult."

"Oh?"

He returned to the bedroom, got into the bed and pulled Ellen close and held her until he could feel her warm thighs and stomach against his. Her eyes were closed and he felt her

169

body warmth like a blanket, a blanket of feelings soothing him.

"You're strange sometimes," she said, opening her eyes and looking at him.

"I do some strange things, too." He was thinking about the bust. He hadn't even told her yet.

"Want to tell me?"

"Not right now."

"Then say you love me," she whispered.

"Why?"

"So I can say it to you."

Later they dressed and put a new sheet on Ellen's bed. Alex stashed the stained one in the trunk of his car, to be dumped on the way home. Gunther wouldn't miss it.

Ellen was on the phone when he returned from the car so he went into the room by the sea and watched the waves roll in. He imagined himself surfing on them, although he had never been on a board. The waves rolled through his life. Some were good waves like Ellen, some were bad waves like Michael. He wondered where he'd be when the rides ended.

"That was Poppa," said Ellen, walking into the room. "It took them longer than they expected to get to the camp. They're going to spend the night in Vermont and drive home tomorrow. He said I should send you home after dinner."

"Oh?" Alex looked at her questioning.

Ellen winked at him. "Wouldn't you like dinner tomorrow morning?"

Alex smiled. "Sure." They hugged each other. Since his arrival it seemed as if they'd spent the day in an embrace.

"He said to expect him around lunchtime tomorrow," Ellen

said. They stood quietly, holding each other. He kissed her again; her eyes were closed.

"Ellen," he said, almost in a whisper, "I've got to tell you about something."

"Hmmm." She was kissing his neck.

"Maybe we ought to take a walk down by the beach," he said, pulling away from her.

She looked concerned. "Is something wrong?"

"Yeah." He nodded. "Not with us, something else, but let's walk first."

They walked out across the back lawn, tasting the sea spray kicked up by the wind. Down by the sand an old dinghy was turned upside down and they sat on it and watched the waves and the sea birds. Alex was looking for something on the beach, but he didn't know exactly what. He knew he had to tell her about the bust, but he still wasn't quite ready.

"What about your prom?" Ellen asked. Her hair was wild in the wind.

"I don't care about it," he said.

"Oh."

He could see that she was disappointed, but with the way things were at Deepbrook High it was better if she didn't go.

"But you'll come to mine?" she asked.

"Sure. When is it?"

"June fifteenth. We're having the Captain Beefheart band, then we're invited to a party. We'll go to the beach the next day, and that night is the senior party."

Aw shit. Taking a smooth sea stone in his hand, Alex stood up and threw it as far out into the ocean as he could. Aw shit, he thought again. He picked up another stone and threw it with all his strength. June sixteenth he had to be in court.

When he turned back toward Ellen, she looked upset. "Alex, what is it?"

"I was . . ." He still couldn't tell her because he was ashamed. He felt that if she knew then he would no longer deserve her. He didn't care what anyone else thought, anyone except Ellen, but he didn't want to do this to her. He was a criminal. She deserved better. He'd already hurt her enough that day. In just a few hours he had botched up her virginity, would have to tell her he couldn't go to her prom, and would stick her with a criminal for a boyfriend.

"I was busted on Wednesday." he said. "I didn't think I'd regret it, but I do and I hate telling you. And I can't go to your prom because I have to go to court the next morning." He reached for her hand and held it tightly. "I'm sorry, Ellen, I really am. You don't deserve this. Here I've ruined your virginity, now you've got a boyfriend who's a criminal and he can't even go to your prom. If you want me to go, I will. I mean, I'll understand perfectly if you don't want to see me anymore. I'm not even sure I want to see myself anymore." He managed to shut up before he said anything dumber than what he'd already said.

Ellen just stared at him.

"Ellen?"

"They're not going to put you in jail, are they?"

Of all the things he had feared she might say, this was not one. "I don't know," he said. "I don't think so."

She stepped inside his arms and hugged him. "Oh, God, Alex," she whispered. For a while they stood quietly holding each other. He listened to the surf and wondered what she could be thinking about.

Then she laughed. He couldn't believe it.

"Oh, Alex, I'm sorry," she said, "it sounds awful, but I just thought, you were busted on Wednesday and I was busted today."

This failed to amuse Alex. He thought she was blaming him. "Ellen, I'm sorry about that, really. I mean, I always thought it was going to be different also. I mean, I screwed it up."

"Alex, you didn't screw it up," Ellen said. "My friend Hildy lost her virginity last fall and she hated it. She bled all over the place and the guy who did it didn't care. I didn't think it was going to be so great. Thank God it wasn't like that."

"Well, I don't know. I thought it would be different."

She reached up and touched his hair. "I know you did. But tell me what happened to you. It must have been awful."

Alex told her. He kept expecting her to get angry at him or start to cry or say something to indicate disgust, but she just listened and now and then asked him to explain something she didn't understand. She wanted to know how his parents reacted and what the kids at school said. Alex found himself telling her his feelings toward the whole situation. He realized he hadn't really been able to talk to anyone else like that.

"You know, until I started talking to you before," he said, "I really thought I didn't care about being busted. I mean, I didn't want to get busted, but when I did I tried to tell myself it didn't matter, but it does."

"Why?" Ellen asked.

"Because it affects you. It means I can't go to your prom."

"Oh, that doesn't matter," she said.

173

"But it does, it sort of represents a lot of things. It affects everybody I know in some way. It makes things harder on them; I mean, even my jerky mother and father. All their friends are going to think they're really idiots for bringing up a kid who goes and gets himself busted."

"But they shouldn't care," Ellen said. "You're not going to do anything like that again. You're really not a criminal. You just made a mistake. It's the kind of thing everybody will look back on someday and shake their heads."

Alex looked away from her and down at the ocean. That was true, and things he could no longer do because of the bust— become a doctor or lawyer—were things he'd never planned to do anyway. Maybe she was right.

TWENTY-NINE

He remembered her falling asleep in his arms, but by the morning they had come undone. He lay quietly, just a few inches from her, listening to her steady soft breaths as she slept. It was the first time he'd spent a whole night with a girl and he marveled at how she could sleep on her stomach, her face buried in the pillow, and not suffocate. Then again, he'd had that same thought the night before as he lay with his full weight on her.

Spending the whole night with her made him feel older. Every time he did something new it was because he hadn't been old enough to do it before. So now he was old enough to spend the night with a woman. In a way, that's what they were all telling him, the cops, Abromowitz, his parents, even Lucille. He was crossing the line again and this time he was glad to do it. With Ellen lying next to him in the bed he felt

175

great. It was idyllic to think of her there beside him. But you couldn't just cross the line in some places and not in others. If he wanted this he had to take the rest.

She moved and he felt her hands reach around him. He pulled her, warm and naked, on top of him. She looked at him with dream-sleepy eyes.

"I love you," she said.

"Yeah, and I love you." He kissed her on the chin.

"I talked to Poppa again about USC," she said. "I think I'm going to go."

Alex suddenly felt fully awake. "He agreed?"

"Not quite, but I don't think he'll stop me."

"Did he get upset?"

"Yes, but I can't be his little girl forever. I guess he's starting to see that."

"You think he'll pay?"

Ellen nodded and her black hair tickled his chest.

"What about us?" Alex said.

"I don't know."

"What do you think?"

"Really, Alex, I don't know," Ellen said softly. "I've never been in love before and I've never gone to college before. What do you think?"

What did he think? That he was crazy about Ellen, but he didn't know if that meant he should go to California or spend the rest of his life with her.

She laid her head on his chest and they didn't say anything more for a while. Alex thought again about the future, aware that it was filled with questions he couldn't answer. What would happen to him because of the bust? Where would he go to college? What would happen to his relationship with Ellen?

For several minutes he lay still, not showing the quiet panic he felt inside. He couldn't go backward and he didn't know what was ahead. That whole year he'd hidden from his future, but now, as James had said, he had to start facing it. Oddly enough, the longer he lay there thinking about it, the less scary the future became. He was even looking forward to going to college because it meant getting away from Deepbrook and the high school. And as far as the bust was concerned, he could only do what Abromowitz had told him and hope for the best. Ellen's taking the news of his arrest so easily made him feel better. Like she'd said, he wasn't really a criminal. And no one seemed to think he would really go to jail. And as for Ellen, well, here she was beside him in bed and they had a whole summer ahead. It was a little premature to start worrying about what could happen to them next fall.

The future, he thought, reaching up to the night table for the box of prophylactics, might not be so bad after all.

"Alex, look!" Alex woke up. Ellen was pointing at the clock beside her bed: 11:30. They must have fallen asleep again. "Poppa said they'd be home around lunchtime." She was already out of the bed and tugging him. "Hurry!"

She piled his clothes into his arms and he tried to get dressed, but it wasn't easy with all those clothes he had to hold. Alex was still not sure whether this was a dream or for real.

"Alex!" she laughed and helped him dress. They got tangled together in his pants and finally he carried his shoes and socks down the stairs. Ellen followed behind him in her bathrobe.

"Would you come to my house next weekend?" he asked on the way down.

"I'll ask Poppa," she said.

She went out the front door with him and into the courtyard. He stopped by the car and they kissed quickly. "I don't understand why you can tell him you're going to California and not to my house," Alex said.

"Because I love him," she said, backing out of his arms and pushing him gently toward the car.

THIRTY

After school on Monday Alex drove to Michael's house and rang the doorbell. He waited a little while and when no one answered he rang it again. Assuming no one was home, Alex was just turning away when the door opened a few inches.

"Who is it?"

It was dark inside and Alex could hardly see the woman except for her face. Michael looked a lot like her. They both had the same long scraggly hair. "My name's Alex Lazar. I'm a friend of Michael's."

Mrs. Martin frowned. "Oh, yes," she said. "He's talked about you. Your mother was the county executive. Michael isn't here." She didn't seem very friendly.

"Yes, I didn't think he would be," Alex said. "I came by because I, uh." Alex actually wasn't sure why he'd come. He didn't expect to find Michael. He wasn't even sure he wanted to find him, but he wanted to understand what had happened, both to him and to Michael. "Because I wanted to find out what happened to him. I'm kind of worried about him."

Michael's mother gave him a long, inquisitive look, as if she were debating whether to let him in, then she opened the door some more and Alex knew he could enter.

He accepted her invitation nervously and stepped inside. He saw at once that she was crippled and needed two metal canes to walk. The air inside smelled stale and acrid with the residue of cigarette smoke. It was worse than Alex had imagined. Somehow he'd pictured a cute little house with brightly painted rooms that were small but cozy. In the tiny dreary kitchen Michael's mother pulled back an old wooden chair with chipped paint and asked Alex to sit at a small Formica table. It was hard to tell what color the walls had been originally; now they were gray and greasy-looking.

"Like something to drink?" Mrs. Martin asked. "Coffee?"

Fearful of what she might serve him and what he might have to drink out of, Alex declined.

"Well, I was just making myself a cup," she said. Alex watched as she poured some water and instant coffee into a cup. Her motions were jittery and uncertain. As she carried the cup to the table about a third of the coffee inside spilled out and into the saucer or on the floor. Alex stood up, thinking he should help, but not sure how.

"Oh, please don't mind," Michael's mother said apologetically. "If I can get from the counter to the table with half a cup I consider it a good day. I have muscular dystrophy." She said this in the frank way only stricken people can speak of themselves. Alex was shaken by the statement, and frightened.

"It's not contagious," she said, as if thinking this was the cause of his concern. She smiled. A sweet smile, Alex thought. She wasn't at all the ogre she first appeared to be.

180

"It's nice to meet you," Mrs. Martin said. Alex could see now that she was uneasy, too.

"Well, actually we've talked on the phone a few times," Alex said.

"Oh, please forgive me if I was nasty," Mrs. Martin said. "But some terrible people call here asking for Michael." Her son's name seemed to make her sad.

"That's one of the reasons I came over," Alex said. "I mean, I wanted to find out what's going on. Michael hasn't been around in a long time." He didn't mention anything about the bust. He had a feeling Michael's mother might not know much, if anything, about her son's involvement.

"I don't know where he is, Alex," Mrs. Martin said.

"When did you hear from him last?"

Mrs. Martin stared down at the tabletop. Her eyes seemed to aim at an old toaster standing in a little sea of bread crumbs. "He came here after he was released from the hospital. To get some things. Clothes, I don't know. He was very angry and said he was going away and would never come back again. I didn't argue. I just don't have the strength for it. I can't keep up with it anymore." Alex sensed that she was forcing herself to say this even though somewhere inside she still cared.

For a while neither of them said anything.

"Well, what's going to happen now?" Alex asked finally.

"What do you mean?" Michael's mother said.

"I mean, do you think Michael will come back?"

"Oh, I'm sorry, Alex," she said. "Michael can't come back anymore. There are disownment proceedings. You see, I have no income except for disability and social security and he is such a financial liability with what he's done and what he still

181

might do. I can't risk it anymore."

"Oh." Alex knew he must have looked shocked.

Mrs. Martin lit a cigarette and dropped the match into an overflowing ashtray. "I'm sorry. You must think that's an awful thing for a mother to do."

"I, uh, don't know. I mean, I know Michael so I guess I can understand it, but I think someday maybe he'll change."

Mrs. Martin inhaled deeply on her cigarette and shook her head slowly. "You tell yourself that for years and then one day it doesn't matter anymore. It's too late to change. There's nothing left."

Later she walked him to the door and thanked him for coming by. He was going to say that he'd let her know if he heard anything about Michael, but he gathered that she preferred not knowing. He drove home. Halfway up the driveway he stopped the car and just sat. The thought of Michael not having a home made him feel like crying. He tried to imagine what it would be like if his parents ever gave up and disowned him.

Across the lawn stood the big white house, his parents' house, symbol of money and success. But it was also his home, the only place he really belonged to.

THIRTY-ONE

Alex's guidance counselor found three colleges that were still accepting students and might be interested in him. Upstate New York, Maine, and Wisconsin were his geographical choices. She wrote down three telephone numbers and told him that when he dialed them he would reach the tennis coaches at the schools in New York and Wisconsin. In Maine he'd speak with the dean of students.

Columbia was not mentioned.

He called the school in Maine first. The dean said that from what the guidance counselor had told them about his grades and SAT scores they would be willing to consider him, but that he would probably be put on academic probation and would not be allowed to go out for any sports until his grade average was acceptable. The dean also told Alex that the school's tennis team had finished in last place in its conference for the last two years in a row.

When he called the tennis coaches at the Wisconsin and New

York schools, they both told him they had teams contending for their conference titles and they would be glad to have him join their squads. Their sales pitches included tutoring in his weak subjects paid for by the athletic department, high-paying part-time jobs if money was a problem, and other "fringe benefits."

Alex told his guidance counselor the school in Maine was his first choice, but that he'd better apply to the school in New York also because Abromowitz had warned him that he might not be allowed to leave the state.

Leaving the guidance counselor's office, Alex practically walked into Principal Seekamp, who was stepping out of his office next door. This was their first meeting since the bust and Alex was wary of the principal, certain that Seekamp, with his latent military mentality, would be rough on him.

"Hello, Alex, I hope you're managing all right," the principal said.

"Thanks."

Seekamp looked around and seeing that they were alone outside the office, he said, "Heard you cleaned up your act before this happened. Bad luck, huh?"

Alex half nodded, half shrugged. *C'est la vie,* wasn't that what they said?

The principal rubbed his eleven-o'clock shadow. "How're you getting along with Miss Mormon?"

"Okay, I guess." There was one more test, a big paper, and the final, and Alex figured if he could get B's on all of them he could finish the year with a C.

"Clear up that chariot business?" the principal asked.

"Chariot? Oh, yes, all cleared up," Alex said.

Principal Seekamp closed his hand over Alex's left shoulder

and gave him an encouraging shake hard enough to rattle some of the fillings in his teeth. "Glad to hear it," he said.

In the library James had taken up residency next to Cindy. "Ah, the rebel who gave up the cause," James said as Alex joined them.

"Hi, Alex," Cindy said.

"Hi, Cindy, what're you up to?" Alex sat down next to James.

"James is telling me about gene pools and the need for diversification in evolution. It's just fascinating."

Alex looked at James. "I'll bet it is."

"Did you know, for instance, that if people with too many similar genes have kids the chances are likely they will reflect their parents genetic weaknesses?" Cindy asked. "That's why there are laws against incest and first cousins marrying."

"No, Cindy, I didn't know that," Alex said. "What you're saying is that in biology, as in physics, opposites should attract." Meanwhile James had picked up a book and appeared to be engrossed in reading.

"Why, yes, I imagine that's so." Cindy looked at James. "Is it?" she asked. James gave no sign that he heard her. "James." Cindy tapped on his book.

"Uh, yes?"

"Would you say that in genetics opposites should attract the way they do in physics?"

James pondered the question a moment. "I suppose it depends on who you're talking to. There's some disagreement among the experts."

Alex groaned.

James pushed his chair back and got up. "Would you excuse us, Cindy. Alex and I have to discuss something, don't we?"

185

"Sure, James." Alex stood up. "Nice talking to you again, Cindy. You know what they say about genes, don't you?"

"No, what?"

"You can't keep a good chromosome down."

Cindy stared at him. "You're strange," she said. James started to tug Alex away by the sleeve.

"Well, you see that's because my mother and father are actually closely related," Alex said. "In fact, they share the same son.".

"Very strange," Cindy said.

James and Alex walked to the book stacks. "What are you trying to do?" James asked. Alex had never seen his friend so emotionally charged over something so silly.

"James, just because she hasn't taken biology doesn't mean you can feed her false information."

"Whose feeding her false information?" James whispered. "I was only presenting the various sides of the genetics story to her."

"Only you forgot the correct side," Alex said.

James shrugged. "A minor oversight when you consider the ultimate goal."

"Are you proceeding?"

"Slowly. I've been trying to think of a good date for this weekend. If I can just come up with something so terrific, so fantastic that she'll want to go no matter who's taking her, I think I'll be safe."

"Well, I've invited Ellen over for the weekend. You want to double with us if she comes? I don't know how terrific or fantastic it will be, but I hope it beats taking her to the Deepbrook Triple–X movies."

James nodded. "I didn't think she'd go for the Triple–X

186

either, although it would be a truly educational experience."

Alex sighed.

"Anyway," James said, "the weather's been lovely and I feel a strange inclination to exercise. Feel like hitting a few tennis balls with me after school?"

"How about tomorrow?"

"Agreed, meet you in the gym."

When Alex got home that night the garage was dark. He flicked the switch that turned on the lights and closed the motorized garage door.

"Alex!"

The hiss of his name startled him. Alex swung around to find Michael lurching toward him, his eyes wide and desperate.

"Don't tell anyone I'm here, Alex. They'll get me," Michael pleaded.

"Calm down, Michael." Alex patted his shoulder. A faint odor hit his nose. Michael probably hadn't changed his clothes in a week.

"Gimme a cigarette," Michael said. Alex gave him one. "They're after me," Michael said, a frantic tinge in his voice. "I don't know what to do." He grabbed Alex's arm. "It's not my fault, Alex." Michael sniffed and coughed and started to sob.

Alex was stunned. He wasn't certain if Michael was acting or serious. Not sure what to do, Alex leaned against the car and waited as the wave of tears washed through Michael's eyes. His face looked bony, and Alex could see that he'd lost more weight since their last meeting.

When the crying stopped, Alex was the first to speak. "Michael, did you get me busted?"

"No," Michael sniffed.

"But Paul was a cop."

"I didn't know until later, I swear I didn't know. They're trying to get me." Michael pawed him again.

"Cut it out, Michael." Alex pushed the hands away. He knew Michael was lying. But what difference did it make now whether he had turned Alex in? Neither of them could do anything to change that. Michael had always been a punk and a liar not to be trusted and Alex could only wonder why he had ever been so dumb as to think he could trust the kid. He no longer looked at Michael as a friend but only as someone he knew, someone who was in trouble.

"Please don't let them, Alex, please." Michael really was acting crazy.

"Who?"

"Everyone," Michael panted. "Chicken and his friends, the cops."

"What?"

Michael told a weird story in broken sentences that sounded only half rational to Alex. He and Paul had gone to Chicken's, there'd been a fight. Michael showed Alex dirty scabs and bruises he said he got in the fight. He'd climbed out a window. Chicken and his friends thought Michael was working with the cops. The cops thought Michael had purposely tried to get Paul killed.

Alex got Michael to sit down. "It's okay, it's really okay," he said, not knowing whether it was or not. Michael started sobbing again. Alex was sure now that he wasn't faking. "Listen, Michael," he said, "you must be hungry. Can I get you something to eat?"

Michael grabbed his arm. "You're not gonna call the cops, are you? You're not gonna turn me in."

188

"No," Alex said, trying to calm him. "You'll feel better if you eat something. I'll come right back."

Alex went through the door from the garage to the hallway that led to the kitchen. Of course Michael had been afraid I'd turn him in, Alex thought. After all, Michael had experience in turning people in. Alex didn't know what to do. Michael was behaving like a cornered animal. Michael *was* a cornered animal. He couldn't go to Chicken, he couldn't go to the police, he couldn't go to school and he couldn't go home. In the kitchen Alex saw that his place was set at the table and a glass of tomato juice had been poured. Lucille must have gone upstairs while waiting for him to come home for dinner. Alex went quickly to the refrigerator and grabbed a package of cold cuts and a bottle of orange juice. From the pantry he took a handful of bread and returned to the garage.

Michael was ravenous. He ate everything. After he finished he wanted to smoke some of Alex's grass. Alex told him he didn't think it was a good idea, but Michael got so weird, demanding, begging, threatening, that Alex went out and dug up the jar and got him some of the remaining grass. Michael consumed the grass just as compulsively as he had the food, taking deep toke after deep toke. When he finished the grass he took three red pills from a plastic container and washed them down with the last of the orange juice. Alex had seen the pills before. They were downers. Then Michael grubbed another cigarette and leaned back and smoked silently.

"I'll have to go back inside and eat dinner or Lucille will know something funny is going on," Alex said.

Michael appeared not to hear him.

"Michael?"

"Yeah, go." Michael said, as if Alex were bothering him.

189

Alex left, not showing his anger. Not a word of thanks from Michael. He'd fed him, given him dope, was taking a chance by hiding him in the garage, and Michael couldn't even show a shred of appreciation.

After dinner, Alex went back to the garage. A strong, sickening stench hit his nose as he opened the door. The smell of vomit. Alex turned on the light. Michael's dinner lay on the concrete floor between Alex's and his mother's cars. Michael was curled up in the corner, his head on an old tire, fast asleep.

Alex's understanding of drug abuse and addiction was less than thorough, but he knew that besides everything else that was wrong, Michael was physically unwell. It might be the drugs, or he might be sick or maybe his mental condition had deteriorated to the point where he was just too nuts to hold anything down. Most likely it was a combination of all three. Alex realized that Michael wasn't going to get well by staying in the garage or running away again.

There were some old blankets lying in a corner and Alex took one, shook it out and laid it over Michael. Then he turned off the light and left the garage. He'd clean up the mess tomorrow when it wasn't quite so pungent. Michael would probably sleep through the night anyway.

For almost an hour he wandered through his house aimlessly, sometimes stopping to sit in one room or another, preoccupied with thoughts of Michael and his predicament. There were not many choices really, and almost from the minute Alex had started thinking about it he knew what the probable decision would be. Michael had to have help, perhaps he'd have to go into the hospital again. Maybe Chicken's friends really were looking for him. He had to be protected,

190

from himself as much as anyone else. It all meant one thing. Either directly or indirectly Alex had to turn him in. He did not doubt that if he took Michael to a doctor or a hospital the police would find him quickly. That much he knew. When the police were looking for someone, the first thing they did was notify places like hospitals.

Besides, the kid had no place else to go. If Michael did leave and something happened to him, Alex would always believe he could have prevented it. Of course, there was the possibility that nothing would happen to Michael or that he would disappear and never be heard from again and Alex could pretend he was safe and happy living under an assumed name in Tahiti. Fat chance.

Alex thought about calling James or Abromowitz, but he already knew what they'd say and besides, it was something he'd have to live with so it was something he should decide. He knew he didn't want to make deals with the police. He didn't want to be an informant. He knew he could use Michael to bargain with the police. If they wanted Michael badly enough, and it seemed they did, then he could probably get them to agree to drop some of the charges in return for telling them where Michael was. Certainly that would happen if he told Abromowitz what was going on. And in a way Michael deserved it, an eye for an eye, a squeal for a squeal. Michael knew all about turning his friends in to save his own skin, but Alex wouldn't do that to anyone, not even to him.

THIRTY-TWO

Alex was up early. He'd had trouble falling asleep and had dreamed about Michael and Ellen. It was the strangest dream—he'd gone to Ellen's house. Michael was there with Ellen and they were kissing and holding hands. He tried to get to them but suddenly he was on Gunther's sailboat sailing away while Michael and Ellen remained on shore, oblivious to him.

He got dressed and went downstairs to the garage. The stale stench of vomit still hung in the air and made Alex want to vomit himself. Michael was still asleep, but his brow was wet, and sweaty hair stuck to his forehead. He was very pale.

He shook Michael's shoulder and the kid jumped as if a cherry bomb had gone off next to his ear. "It's me, Alex."

"Oh," Michael moaned and didn't get up. His face was smudged with black dirt from the tire. "I feel sick."

"Come on, Michael, get up." For some reason Alex thought that if Michael could stand up it would mean he was okay.

"No, gimme some water, I'm thirsty." Michael's voice was weak. He looked like he was in agony.

192

Alex left and returned with a large glass of water. Michael drank it as though he were pouring it straight down his throat. Both his hands trembled as he held the glass. "Gimme more," he said.

"No, that's too much water. It'll make you sick."

"Some fuckin' friend you are," Michael whined.

"The only one you've got, jerk," Alex said angrily. At that moment if Michael had said he wanted to leave, Alex would have gladly helped him go.

Michael pushed himself up to a sitting position and bent over holding his stomach. "I'm sick." He grimaced.

Alex went to get some aspirin and cigarettes. Michael gobbled the aspirin but he could only take two puffs from the cigarette before he dropped it on the floor, saying he couldn't smoke anymore. For a while Alex sat on the floor near Michael and smoked one of the cigarettes. Michael lay down again. He looked terrible—thin and dirty and sweaty. He was the palest person Alex had ever seen; his skin almost had a gray tint. Alex just sat and watched while Michael lay still, curled up on the floor with his arms around his stomach.

Alex felt a sadness growing in him. Before him lay the remains of the mighty Michael Martin. The tough, big dealer was now a skinny, scared, sniveling kid hiding in Alex's garage from the police and assorted bogeymen. In a way, Michael had done Alex a favor, he'd shown Alex what the whole drug scene was like, he'd shown Alex what could happen. Were it not for Michael, Alex might never have known. Were it not for Michael, Alex himself might have been hiding and sick on someone's garage floor in a few months.

It was almost time for Lucille to come down to the kitchen and make breakfast. Alex went back inside one last time and

193

refilled the glass. Then he left some more aspirin with Michael, telling him he'd come back right after school, and they'd figure out what to do. But he knew he was lying.

He couldn't do it. Not after first period. Not after second. After third period he looked upward to the Great Nothing and asked for help. As usual he got no reply. Fourth, fifth and sixth periods passed. Useless. It made no sense to wait. Michael couldn't run forever. The way he looked that morning Alex wasn't sure he could run at all.

Finally, after seventh period, his last of the day, Alex walked to the phone booth outside Seekamp's office. He had to make the call, not because he'd decided, but because he was going crazy trying to decide.

He looked up the number of the county police and dialed.

"County, Sergeant Dumas."

"Can I speak to Lieutenant Dougherty, please?"

"Hold on."

"Hello?"

"Lieutenant Dougherty?"

"You got him."

"This is Alex Lazar."

"Hello, Alex, what can I do for you?"

"Michael Martin is in my garage."

"Now?"

"Yes."

"Is he armed?"

"I don't think so."

"Okay, Alex, thanks." Dougherty hung up.

C'est la vie, baby.

From the office Alex went to the gym where James was

waiting to play tennis. The gnome was unusually quiet. "What's wrong?" Alex asked.

"I proposed the double date, but Cindy declined," James said. "She said she thought it was best if we remained friends."

"I'm sorry, James."

"It's okay, it wouldn't have worked out anyway."

"Genes?" Alex asked.

"Yeah, but I don't mind," James said philosophically. "Some of us possess an outward beauty, but it can be superficial. Others, like myself, have an inward beauty. Something like a geode. I know I've got it where it counts."

They walked out to the tennis courts and talked as they hit a few tennis balls back and forth.

"James, I'm sorry it didn't work out."

"Yeah." The curly head bobbed up and down. "Hey, I saw an ad in the paper this morning. The Deepbrook Tennis Club is looking for an assistant pro for the summer."

"Thanks, James, I'll check it out." Despite what James had said about geodes, Alex knew what he was probably thinking—that if he had tall good-looking genes Cindy might have said yes when he asked her out. It wasn't fair. If anyone didn't deserve good genes it was Alex. Here he had them and he didn't even appreciate them. Alex thought about Michael's mother, crippled, sitting alone in that dark musty house, and he thought about Michael, practically crazy. Maybe, in some ways, he was lucky he'd been born Alex Lazar, son of Carla and Edward, and not Michael Martin or even James Lasky. Most of the people would have given anything to have his genes. And even if Carla and Edward had done a pretty crappy job as parents, he'd be on his own one of these days and it wouldn't matter much.

It was almost too dark to play any longer, but Alex asked James if he felt like hitting a few more.

"Not unless they install lights in the tennis balls," James said. He was right, but Alex didn't want to get off the court. He knew he was afraid to go home and see what had happened to Michael.

"Come on, Alex," James said. "Let's go home."

The sky was turning darker by the second. Alex stood in the middle of the tennis court, looking upward, feeling utterly alone. Even with James a few feet away and Ellen just an hour away, he was alone. He had heard that saying, *You come into the world alone and you go out alone,* and there were times, like right now, when no amount of friends and girlfriends and parents could hide him from the nothingness out there. The Great Nothing. No one to tell him what to do, no one to tell him if what he'd already done was right or wrong. He alone had decided to turn Michael in.

"Alex!" Someone shouted his name. Alex turned and saw Principal Seekamp running toward him. "We just got a call from your house," the principal yelled. "The police want you home right away."

THIRTY-THREE

James went with Alex. As they neared Upper Deepbrook, they saw a crowd of people outside the entrance. A police car, its bubble flashing red and blue, blocked the stone gates, and several cops stood near the car, preventing anyone from going through. Alex stopped his car and was getting out when one of the cops saw him and hurried over. "You Alex Lazar?" he asked.

Alex nodded.

"Okay, get in your car and come through." The cop walked in front of the car clearing a path and Alex followed. He and James looked at each other uncomfortably as the faces peered in at them. The faces were ugly, they resented the intrusion. Alex knew they were wondering who in the car thought himself so important that he could drive through. Alex wanted to ignore the faces, but he couldn't. They were all looking, gesturing, pointing.

"I can't believe the crowd out here," Alex said, driving carefully.

"I can," James said. "They want to see blood. This is better than television."

"But they can't see anything out here."

"Doesn't matter, they can feel it. They can smell trouble in the air. It's the vulture syndrome. Our scavenger carnivore instincts. They're here to pick every juicy detail off the bones. It's the roller coasters."

"Come off it," Alex said.

"No, it is. These civilized people, they never get close enough to death anymore. They never have anything to compare life to, so life loses its meaning after a while. Out here they feel alive because they can sense death. That's what a roller coaster is, a mechanical death trip. Scares the shit out of people and they love it because it makes them feel alive. Vicarious thrills. That's what Evel Knievel's all about."

"I could live without *this* thrill," Alex said.

When they got inside the gates the cop stopped them and leaned in the window. "Don't know for sure what's going on," he said. "An ambulance just went in. Park so you won't block it."

Alex thanked the cop and drove quickly down Meadow Lark Lane. They heard the sirens just as they came around the bend in front of the house. The ambulance lights flashing, siren howling, turned out of his driveway and flew past them.

With James behind him, Alex ran up the path and into the house. There were some cops standing around talking and the sounds of a woman crying. The cops stared at Alex, but said nothing. He looked in the living room. Lucille was sitting on the couch crying. As Alex watched, a young man wearing a white jacket bent over her and gave her a shot in the arm.

Alex turned to the cops and asked what had happened. "Talk to Dougherty," one of them said, pointing upstairs.

The door to his parents' room was open and inside, Alex found Dougherty. The room was a mess, drawers pulled open and clothes dumped out. As Alex stepped into the room he felt something crack under his foot. He reached down and picked up the pieces of a plastic pill bottle. About half a dozen similar bottles, all open, some empty, some with a few pills still inside, lay loose on the floor.

When he looked up, Dougherty was watching him. The detective looked sad.

"Michael?" Alex asked, suddenly realizing what must have happened.

Dougherty nodded.

THIRTY-FOUR

They called it an accidental overdose. Michael had lost track of what he was taking. He'd gotten so stoned he'd forgotten that his stomach was full of pills and had taken more.

"You understand what that means," Dougherty was saying. "It was an accident. No one is at fault." They were sitting in Dougherty's office in the county center. Dougherty knew what Alex was thinking, that it was his fault, that he could have prevented what happened by calling sooner, that he could have put Michael in a car and taken him to a hospital instead of going to school and procrastinating all day.

Three days had passed since Michael was taken to the hospital in a coma. He had not yet waked up and the doctors weren't sure when or if he ever would. Dougherty told Alex that Michael had gone into the house looking for drugs. Hearing noises, Lucille had gone into the bedroom and found Michael already staggering. Michael had tried to attack her, although no one was sure why. A blood test found phency-clidine, angel dust, in Michael's blood. Dougherty said cases of irrational violence were becoming more and more common with the drug. Lucille had escaped and sought help at the rent-a-cop station. The police were called. They were there ahead of Dougherty.

Alex and James had spent a good part of the night cleaning the house, basically because Alex didn't know what else to do and he didn't want to be alone. The doctor had given Lucille a sedative and she was fast asleep.

After the cleaning was finished, James and Alex sat in the kitchen silently, except for one short conversation about Michael, about whether he would have destroyed himself one way or another before too long, and about Alex's responsibility to Michael. James wouldn't discuss what might have happened had Alex handled it differently. He said Alex had to deal with what had happened, not what could have happened.

When James finally couldn't stay up any longer and had gone into the den to lie down, Alex stepped out on the porch in the back of the house and sat in the dark. The tears were overdue, but they came, for Michael. And he knew he was crying for himself, too, and for all the dumb mistakes he'd made and all the dumb things he'd done. Maybe James was right when he said that sooner or later Michael would have wound up in a coma in a hospital bed. But Alex remembered the day they'd bought the dust and how he'd almost refused to buy it. Now he wished he had refused. Now he wished he'd never gotten involved in dealing at all.

A seething Abromowitz had called the next morning. "Why didn't you call me last night?" he asked angrily. "The only way I found out anything had happened was when the DA called this morning. What the hell am I supposed to tell your parents?"

"Nothing," Alex had said.

"What?"

Alex paused for a second before answering again. Was that what he really wanted? Yes, it was. "Nothing," he said again. "Don't even call them."

He had cleaned up the house. The pill prescriptions would be refilled. His parents' presence was not necessary. His life as a low-maintenance offspring had come to a close. From now on he would require no maintenance except that which he could administer to himself. He would make his own decisions about where he would go to college and what he would study and what he would do afterward.

Despite all that had happened his feelings toward his parents hadn't changed much. The difference from before was he knew he didn't have to act to spite or rebel against them anymore. He didn't feel he had to prove anything to them. They knew and he knew he could act on his own. Everybody had to prove it to himself once. He did it by dealing drugs and getting busted. That was all the proving he intended to do for a long time.

In his office Dougherty leaned toward Alex. "It's not your fault," he said again. "They ought to classify this damn angel dust as a narcotic. It's too damn dangerous."

Alex nodded. Dougherty would blame the drugs, but not the circumstances that prompted kids like Michael, and even himself, to take them.

"I also feel that you've cooperated with us," the detective said. "I'm going to recommend to the DA that the charges against you be reduced."

Alex forced a smile on to his face and thanked him. Talk about ironies.

Later he walked out of the county center, past the spot where a few weeks before he'd been pulled, handcuffed, from the detectives' car. He was eager to get home, Ellen would be arriving in a few hours and they were finally going to have a weekend in Deepbrook together. But at the car he paused for a moment and imagined Michael sitting in the front seat, smoking and flicking his ashes on the floor. It was all over. He had crossed the line for good. Why he made it and Michael hadn't he didn't know. Alex looked up at the sky. Only the Great Nothing really knew. That asshole.